'Is this so **snobbery th** **acknowled** **friends, Mr Hammond?'**

She saw Barnabas raise his eyebrows at her plain speaking, but he did not seem in any way taken aback and he answered her without prevarication.

'Not at all. The truth is I prefer not to tell anyone. Were my father to know, I fear he would take shameless advantage.'

Lavender turned aside. She felt a little embarrassed. She knew exactly what he meant. Arthur Hammond was such a social climber that he would be beside himself with excitement to discover that Barnabas had such upper-class friends.

'Have you kept this a secret for all these years, then?' she asked, unable to prevent her curiosity surfacing again.

'Oh, it is but one of many secrets!' Barnabas said easily.

**A young woman disappears.
A husband is suspected of murder.
Stirring times for all the neighbourhood in**

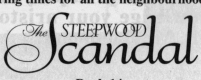

The STEEPWOOD
Scandal

Book 14

When the debauched Marquis of Sywell won
Steepwood Abbey years ago at cards, it led to the death
of the then Earl of Yardley. Now he's caused scandal
again by marrying a girl out of his class—and young
enough to be his granddaughter! After being married
only a short time, the Marchioness has disappeared,
leaving no trace of her whereabouts. There is every
expectation that yet more scandals will emerge, though
no one yet knows just how shocking they will be.

The four villages surrounding the Steepwood Abbey
estate are in turmoil, not only with the dire goings-on
at the Abbey, but also with their own affairs. Each
story in **The Steepwood Scandal** follows the mystery
behind the disappearance of the young woman, and the
individual romances of lovers connected in some way
with the intrigue.

**Regency Drama
intrigue, mischief...and marriage**

AN UNLIKELY SUITOR

Nicola Cornick

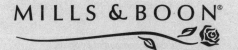

First published in Great Britain 2002
Harlequin Mills & Boon Limited,
Eton House, 18-24 Paradise Road, Richmond, Surrey TW9 1SR

© Harlequin Books S.A. 2002

Special thanks and acknowledgement are given to Nicola Cornick
for her contribution to The Steepwood Scandal series.

ISBN 0 263 82855 7

Set in Times Roman 10½ on 12½ pt.
119-0602-55085

Printed and bound in Spain
by Litografia Rosés S.A., Barcelona

Nicola Cornick is passionate about many things: her country cottage and its garden, her two small cats, her husband and her writing—though not necessarily in that order! She has always been fascinated by history, both as her chosen subject at university and subsequently as an engrossing hobby. She works as an university administrator and finds her writing the perfect antidote to the demands of life in a busy office.

An Unlikely Suitor features characters you will have already met in *A Companion of Quality*, Nicola Cornick's previous novel in **The Steepwood Scandal.**

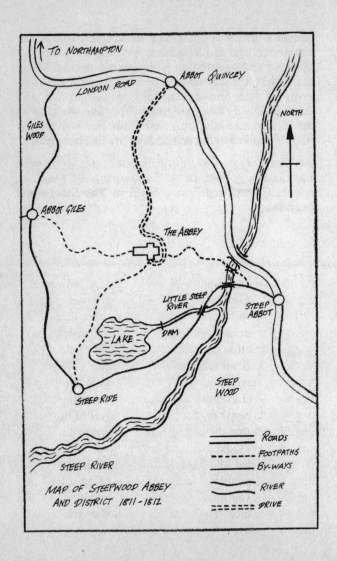

TO NORTHAMPTON

LONDON ROAD

ABBOT QUINCEY

GILES WOOD

NORTH

ABBOT GILES

THE ABBEY

LITTLE STEEP RIVER

STEEP ABBOT

LAKE

DAM

STEEP WOOD

STEEP RIDE

STEEP RIVER

MAP OF STEEPWOOD ABBEY
AND DISTRICT 1811 - 1812

ROADS
FOOTPATHS
BY-WAYS
RIVER
DRIVE

Chapter One

September 1812

'Just how many pairs of gloves does a lady need, Lavender?' Caroline Brabant asked her sister-in-law.

The two of them were sitting in the library at Hewly Manor, a long elegant room lined with walnut bookshelves that the Admiral, Lavender's father, had stocked with all manner of fascinating collections from his travels abroad. Caroline was reclining on the sofa and Lavender had just finished reading aloud to her from *Sense and Sensibility,* a novel of manners and morals that they were both enjoying.

Lavender looked up from the book. Caroline's query sounded idle but Lavender knew that she seldom asked pointless questions. Nor, being a lady of quality, did Caroline need Lavender's advice on matters of elegance. There had to be another reason for the question…

'I am not sure, Caro,' she began carefully. 'Three or four, perhaps? A best and second best pair and a pair for evenings—'

Caroline sighed and put aside her magazine. 'Hammonds the drapers must find you quite their best customer then,' she observed gently, 'for by my calculations, you have bought no less than six pairs of gloves in the last quarter alone!'

Lavender avoided her eyes. Caroline was disconcertingly shrewd.

'If not gloves then bonnets, scarves or materials…' Caroline was saying now. 'Have all your clothes worn out at the same time, Lavender?'

Lavender jumped up and crossed to the library window. Dusk was falling across Hewly Manor gardens and it was time to light the candles. She kept her back to Caroline and tried to speak casually.

'You know how it may be, Caro…' She was proud of the lightness of her tone. 'Sometimes everything seems to need replacing at once! Now that it is autumn again I find I have a need for some new items, warmer clothes to suit the weather—' She broke off, aware that she was starting to ramble and sure that she could feel Caroline's intent gaze riveted on the back of her head. Usually she was delighted to have Caroline's companionship and felt that her brother Lewis could not have made a better match. Usually, but not today. Not when Caroline was in the kind of mood to press her on her new-found interest in drapery.

'I think I shall take a walk before dark,' she said hastily, feeling the need to escape Caroline's shrewd eye. 'I have the headache and a brisk stroll around the gardens may help…'

Caroline picked up the needlework that lay beside her on the rose brocade sofa. 'Very well. I shall not offer to accompany you, for I find I tire so easily these days.' She tilted her head to consider the baby clothes that she was embroidering with such enviable skill. 'I believe I shall be in need of some more thread tomorrow. Perhaps you would be so good as to walk into Abbot Quincey and purchase some for me, Lavender?'

Lavender shot her a suspicious look, but Caroline's face was serene as she bent over her work. Now that she was increasing, there was an air of contentment about her that Lavender thought was even more marked than in the first days of her marriage to Lewis. Unfortunately for Lavender, Caroline's pregnancy had affected neither the quickness of her mind nor her powers of observation.

Lavender closed the library door softly behind her. She could hear a bell ringing in the depths of the house as Caroline called for the candles to be lit, and a housemaid scurried out of the servants' quarters, dropped Lavender a curtsey and gave her a smile, before hastening to do the mistress's bidding.

Lavender had been quick to see that all the servants liked Caroline. There was such an air of peace about Hewly these days, though Caroline joked that all that would be ruined once the baby was born.

Lavender went to fetch her coat and boots from the garden room. The house was spick and span, though giving the impression of being a little frayed at the edges. There was little spare money for refurbishment, for Lewis was ploughing it all back into the estate in order to repair the neglect of the last few years. Lavender did not mind—she found Hewly's worn elegance comforting and tasteful, and besides, she knew that whilst they were still in mourning for her father it would not be appropriate to begin a major restoration. Lewis had hinted that they might go up to Town the following autumn, but Lavender hoped that they would not. She had endured one tedious London Season four years before and had no wish to be bored by another. Yet it did raise the spectre of her future, for now that Lewis was married and with a family on the way she did not wish to hang on his coat-tails. Neither he nor Caroline would ever give the impression that she was an unwelcome third, but even so…

Lavender went out of the front door and paused for a moment on the gravel path, trying to decide which way to go. Before her, the formal parterre led to the walled gardens and beyond that to the orchard. She could see the moon rising through the branches of the apple trees. She drew on one of the many pairs of gloves that Caroline had referred to, and started to walk along the path.

Perhaps, Lavender thought as she walked, she could become one of those redoubtable maiden aunts upon whom every family depended. As Lewis and Caroline's brood expanded she could be an additional nursery nurse and governess, indispensable to servants and family alike. Everyone would remark on how good she was with the children and how they doted on her. As she grew older she could become eccentric, buy herself a cottage and keep cats. She would have her painting and her botany…

Lavender's pace slowed. The truth was that the thought left her with a hollow feeling somewhere inside her. She had every intention of being a devoted aunt to Lewis and Caroline's children, but what if she wished for a family of her own? She was unhappily aware that at three and twenty she was well past marriageable age and that she had never met a man who made her pulse race. Well, if she were honest, she had met one, and that was the root of the whole trouble…

She reached the orchard and stopped for a moment whilst the wind snatched the fallen leaves from the path and whirled them around her. The sky was a clear, dark blue and it promised to be a chilly night. It was September, one of Lavender's favourite months, but already she could feel the year turning, echoing her own feeling of passing time.

On impulse she let herself out through the door in the wall and found herself in the cobbled street that led from the Manor down to the Steep River, past the Guarding Academy. She had not intended to walk far, but now that darkness was falling a sudden inclination took her down to the water, along the Abbey wall and to the edge of the woods. In the daylight Lavender wandered far and wide with no concerns for distance or safety but it was not so sensible to do so at night. She had heard that there were poachers in the woods, and whilst she thought they would not hurt her, it was best not to be seen. Lavender shivered a little in the sharp breeze. She had seen and heard plenty of odd things in the time that she had lived in Steep Abbot, but she never told a soul…

She passed the Guarding Academy and smiled a little as she heard the faint sound of singing on the air. Tonight must be choir practice. The music followed her down to the river, where it was lost amongst the noise of the tumbling water. The moon was a silver disc on the rippling surface and the wind hummed in the trees.

There was a short cut along the edge of the woods back to the Manor gardens, a little path that was bordered on one side by a stone wall and had the whispering trees on the other. It was only a step back to the Hewly estate, but for some reason Lavender felt unexpectedly nervous. Telling herself that it was hunger and not fear that rumbled in her stomach, she stepped out boldly.

She had gone only four paces when she almost stumbled over a large sack that was lying at the side of the path. She looked around hastily, but there was no one in sight. The shadows were thick beneath the trees and the leaves rustled. She could still hear the sound of the river running, for it was only a few yards behind her.

Gooseflesh crept along Lavender's skin. She could not decide what to do. She could retrace her steps and go home the way she had come, or she could pass by, pretending that she had noticed nothing. That was surely better than opening the sack and discovering some choice piece of game that a poacher was about to reclaim. Then she thought she heard a sound from inside the bag and in spite of her better judgement, she bent down. She had just stretched her hand towards it, when the whole sack shifted of its own accord, as though possessed. Lavender let out an involuntary scream.

Immediately there was a step behind her on the path and before she could even stand up, someone grabbed her arm and spun her round.

Lavender found herself in the rough embrace of someone who clearly wished to prevent her from screaming again. One of his arms was tight about her waist and the coarse material of his coat scored her cheek. He was very tall. And broad. Her hands were pressed against his chest and she was conscious of the hard muscle beneath her fingers and the steady beat of his heart.

Curiously this discovery led Lavender to become acutely aware of the information her senses were providing. She could hear the rustle of the trees mingled with her assailant's breathing, feel the cold touch of the breeze and the warmth of his skin as he bent his head and his cheek brushed her hair. And he smelled wonderful, a mixture of cold air and the faint tang of citrus. It was this last impression that somehow weakened her and she felt her legs tremble and his arm tighten about her in response.

'Mr Hammond!'

Lavender could not have said how she knew his identity but she had no doubts at all, and the words were out before she even had time to think. She pushed a little shakily against the man's chest and he let go of her at once, stepping back so that he was facing her, a few steps away.

'Miss Brabant!' Barnabas Hammond's voice was as slow and thoughtful as she remembered, but warmed now by an amusement that Lavender felt was surely out of place. She had always liked the way that Barney spoke, with perfect courtesy but no hint of deference. His father was always obsequious towards his upper-class clients in the draper's shop, and Lavender found this grated on her, particularly when she had seen his dismissive scorn towards the poorer customers. She had observed that Barney always treated everybody in exactly the same way and had liked him for it.

Now, however, she felt oddly at a loss, as though the clear definition of their relationship had somehow been blurred. He was a shopkeeper's son and she was an admiral's daughter, and with the shop counter between them she had allowed herself to dream a little. He might always speak to everyone in the same manner, but there was a decided hint of warmth when he addressed her, an admiration in his eyes that had made her heart beat a little faster. Then he had been so kind to her when her father had died. He scarcely knew her and yet his words of comfort had been so perceptive.

Caroline was right—she had been calling in at the draper's shop more often of late, contriving an order of ribbons here, a pair of gloves there. She blushed to think of it now. She had thought… But here her thoughts became at the best confused. Was she a snob, aware of her status and the relative inferiority of his, or was she above such things, scornful of those whose lives were ruled by rank and privilege? Whatever the case, she had never met Barnabas Hammond in a situation such as this and it made her feel strangely vulnerable.

The odd effect he had on her caused her voice to

come out with decidedly squeaky overtones when she would have preferred to sound authoritative.

'Mr Hammond, what do you mean by creeping around in the dark—and with *this*—' She gestured with her foot towards the offending sack. It seemed obvious that he had been poaching and worse, that his quarry was still alive.

'I would have thought better of you!' she finished with self-righteous indignation.

'Would you?' Barney Hammond sounded surprised and amused. 'Naturally, I am flattered, Miss Brabant, but why should you?'

Lavender frowned slightly. She could not see his expression properly, for it was almost full dark now and besides, he was possessed of a face that was inscrutable at the best of times. She had heard the maids giggling over Barney Hammond, remarking on his good looks and athletic physique, and whilst Lavender would have said that he was in no way classically handsome, she was aware that there was definitely something about him. It was a something that made her feel quite hot and bothered when she dwelt on it and it had even led Caroline once to remark, completely dispassionately, that she could see why all the village girls were wild for him.

Lavender tried to concentrate, aware that such thoughts were making matters worse rather than better. She knew that it would be best to make her excuses and leave, but Barney was waiting politely for her response and she felt it would be rude simply to walk away.

'I did not imagine that you would stoop to poaching,' she said coldly, indicating the sack again. It had not moved again but she knew she had not imagined it. 'And to take your prey without killing it cleanly—that is rank cruelty!'

This time she heard him laugh. 'Oh, so you think I am a poacher, Miss Brabant? I see!' The warmth in his tone had slid into teasing and Lavender was even more confused. Not only was this inappropriate, it suggested that he was completely heartless!

'What else am I supposed to think?' she countered angrily, wondering why the timbre of his voice was so attractive when his words were so much the opposite. 'I heard a noise from the sack—and I saw it move! And why else would you be out after dark—'

She watched in amazement as Barney crouched down on the path and loosened the string at the neck of the sack. Suddenly she did not want to see whatever poor, maimed creature was inside.

'I pray you, put it out of its misery quickly,' she said hastily, looking the other way. 'How can you be so unkind—'

'Putting them out of their misery was precisely what my father intended,' Barney said dryly. 'I fear that you have jumped to the wrong conclusions, Miss Brabant.'

Lavender heard a tiny mewing sound and looked

round sharply. Barney was easing something gently out of the sack, something soft, fluffy and with very sharp claws. Lavender saw him wince as the kitten sank teeth and claws simultaneously into his hand.

'Oh, there are two of them!'

'Yes, and not precisely grateful for my clemency!'

Lavender stepped closer and Barney opened his fist to reveal the two tiny bodies. They were shivering a little, peering round with huge-eyed apprehension. Lavender put a hand out and tentatively stroked one tiny head.

'Oh, how adorable! But—' She looked up suddenly into his face. 'The sack—you were going to drown them in the river?'

'My father intended them for such a fate,' Barney corrected her. He was stroking the kittens with gentle fingers and Lavender could hear their ecstatic purrs. 'Their mother was a stray and he did not wish to encourage her, but my sister Ellen had grown much attached to the kittens and begged me to find them a good home. So I offered to take them away and my father assumed I would get rid of them.'

Lavender shivered. 'But what were you intending to do with them? Has someone offered to take them in?'

For the first time, Barney looked a little shifty. 'Not exactly. There is an old byre just up the path and I was intending to make a nest for them there and leave them overnight. I was just collecting bed-

ding for them when you stumbled upon the sack!
Then tomorrow, if I could, I hoped to persuade someone to give them a home…'

Lavender raised her eyebrows. 'That does not
sound a very good plan! They might stray away and
they can scarce be expected to catch their own food,
you know!'

'I brought some scraps of food and some milk with
me,' Barney said, his voice completely expressionless.

Lavender found herself trying not to laugh. It
seemed ridiculous that this man had been devoting
himself so wholeheartedly to the welfare of such tiny
kittens. Yet the little creatures evidently liked him,
for they had subsided into blissful balls of fluff under
the stroking of his hands. Lavender found her mind
making a sudden and unexpected leap from the fate
of the kittens to the caress of Barney's fingers, and
felt herself turn hot all over.

'Do you have any butter with you?' she asked,
somewhat at random. 'If you butter their paws they
will be too busy washing them to think of straying.'

Barney looked crestfallen. 'I did not think of that.
Do you truly think they might lose themselves in the
wood?'

'Cats are homing creatures,' Lavender explained,
glad to be able to speak with authority, 'and they
might try to find their way back to you. But they are
so far from Abbot Quincey they could never make

the journey! Why, they might fall in the river, or become exhausted, or be eaten—'

'Miss Brabant, pray do not distress yourself.' Barney sounded amused and rueful at the same time. 'I am sure they need suffer no such injury—'

'Well, but you cannot know that!' Lavender said indignantly. She took a deep breath. 'I have just the idea—I will take them back to Hewly with me and they may have a home there.' The suggestion seemed to come from nowhere, and startled her almost as much as it seemed to surprise Barney. He stared at her through the dark.

'You will? But—'

'We are forever having problems with mice at the Manor,' Lavender said, improvising hastily in order not to appear too sentimental. 'The kittens will be the very thing to deal with them.'

Barney looked at her. It hardly needed pointing out that the kittens were scarcely bigger than mice themselves.

'They will grow,' Lavender said defensively, as though he had spoken aloud. 'With a little care—'

She put out a hand for the sack, but Barney picked it up and slipped the cats back inside.

'It is very kind of you,' he said slowly. 'If you are certain—'

'Of course! And then you may tell your sister that they have gone to a good home!'

Barney looked at her inscrutably. 'And what will you tell your brother and sister-in-law?'

'Why, that I found the kittens in a sack on the path, just as I did! It would not do to lie, and they know me well enough to know I would not just leave them there!'

Barney swung the sack up. 'I will escort you back to the Manor then, Miss Brabant.'

'There is no need! And if anyone should see you—' Lavender broke off, aware that he might misinterpret her words. She did not wish him to think that she thought herself above his company.

Barney gave her a look, but he did not speak, merely standing back to allow her to precede him along the path. It seemed that her objections had been overruled. Lavender opened her mouth to protest, then closed it again.

They went a little way in silence, then Barney said suddenly, 'So you truly thought me a poacher, Miss Brabant?'

Lavender found herself on the defensive. 'Well, I was not to know! Why else would a man go creeping about the woods in the dark?'

'There could be any number of reasons, I imagine,' Barney said surprisingly. 'I am disappointed that you hold so low an opinion of me, Miss Brabant! I hoped you might think better of me than that!'

The last thing Lavender had expected was to find herself apologising. 'Well, I am truly sorry, but you must allow me some justification. Besides, you made matters considerably worse by manhandling me—' She broke off again. Perhaps it was not wise to remind him of that either. There was a pause.

'Yes, I beg your pardon.' She thought she could detect amusement in his tone again. 'I believe that was purely instinctive, but I apologise for upsetting you.'

Lavender had no intention of admitting that she had been disturbed rather than upset. His proximity and his touch had quite set her senses awry and she was still trembling slightly with the same strange awareness.

They had reached the gap in the wall where the path to Hewly gardens cut across the fields, and she turned to him.

'It would be better if you did not come any further, Mr Hammond. If anyone sees you they will know there is more to my tale than meets the eye.' She took the sack from him. 'Please assure your sister that I will take care of her kittens. Now I'll bid you goodnight.'

Barney stood back and gave her a half-bow, executed as neatly as any of the gentleman of society whom she had met. He then spoiled the effect by giving her a grin, his teeth flashing very white in the moonlight.

'Goodnight, then, Miss Brabant. And thank you.'

He had already melted into the dark as Lavender

turned away to hurry across the fields to home. She found herself wanting to turn and watch him go, which impulse both puzzled and annoyed her. Grasping the kittens to her, she let herself in at the garden gate and steadfastly refused to look back. There was no doubt that Barney Hammond had disturbed her. He had disturbed her very much indeed.

'I cannot believe that you have managed to foist two repellent strays upon this household, Lavender,' Lewis Brabant said testily, as he disentangled one of the kittens from his trouser leg at breakfast the following morning. The little creature, a bundle of ginger fluff, hung on tenaciously. Lewis put his newspaper down and picked it up with a gentleness that belied his words. The kitten started to purr immediately and Lewis pulled a face.

'See how she likes you,' Caroline offered with a smile. She was feeding the other kitten on her lap and it was eating ferociously. 'Poor little scraps—I believe they are half starved!'

Lewis made a noise indicative of disgust. 'Well, they had best start to earn their keep! The kitchen will be the best place for them, not the drawing-room!'

'Yes, my dear,' Caroline said soothingly. She gave him a winning smile. 'They will surely be warm and well fed if we keep them indoors!' Her smile broadened. 'You cannot cozen me—I know you think them delightful.'

Lewis gave a non-committal grunt and got up from the breakfast table. He bent to kiss his wife. 'I shall be in the estate room if you need me. If I find any mice, I shall know what to do!'

Caroline was still smiling as she watched him out of the room. She turned to her sister-in-law. 'I do believe your new pets are a success, Lavender! Lewis is quite smitten!'

Lavender raised her eyebrows. She knew that her brother's disapproval was partly feigned but she had been hard pressed to explain her rescue of the kittens in a convincing fashion. To go out for a walk and return with two new pets in a sack was somewhat singular, especially as she was claiming simply to have found them.

'Is it not strange,' Caroline was musing now, 'that the kittens were wrapped in a sack from Hammond's store? The sort of sacking used to bind up reels of material and the like? I wonder if they have lost them? Perhaps we should ask, for they may wish for them back—'

Lavender jumped, spilling some of her hot chocolate. She had not thought of that.

'Was it one of Hammond's sacks? I did not notice,' she said, as casually as she was able.

'Which reminds me,' Caroline continued, 'that you promised to go to Abbot Quincey for some purchases

for me today. Some embroidery thread, and I find I
need some ribbons as well. I have made a list. Is that
still convenient, Lavender?'

Lavender sighed. It was unfortunate that Caroline
should have a commission for her today of all days.
She did not wish for a walk this morning and she
certainly did not want to go into Abbot Quincey and
into Hammonds drapers shop. Having paid the shop
too many visits in the past month, she now felt a
distinct inclination to stay away from Barnabas
Hammond, a need to avoid all those puzzling and
disturbing feelings that he had brought to the surface.
She had tossed and turned for a good hour before
she had fallen asleep the previous night, and most of
her thoughts had centred on Barney Hammond.

She realised that Caroline was watching her with
bright hazel eyes, and that she had not yet replied.

'It is perfectly convenient, Caro,' she said hastily.
She pushed away her plate of ham and eggs.
Suddenly she did not feel so hungry.

'I must send a message to Lady Perceval as well,'
Caroline said. 'Now, where did I leave the writing
box? In the library? I have become so tiresomely
forgetful of late...'

Lavender smiled. 'Nanny Pryor says that that happens to ladies who are increasing!'

Caroline looked offended. 'What arrant nonsense!'

'Then why are you wearing your thimble for
breakfast, Caro?'

Caroline looked down at her finger and tutted. 'Gracious! I could have sworn that I left that in my sewing bag!' She caught Lavender's eye and smiled reluctantly. 'Very well, you have proved your point! Now, what was it that I was looking for?'

'The writing paper.' Lavender got up hastily. 'I will fetch it for you, Caro! I do not wish you to become lost on your way to the library!'

Chapter Two

The walk into Abbot Quincey was one that Lavender knew particularly well and normally she enjoyed it immensely. She loved the sound of the wind in the tall trees, the shadow patterns of the clouds as they raced across the fields and the sting of the fresh air in her face. Her walks always gave her ample time to think about her painting and her reading and any number of other delightful and intellectual pursuits that had always filled her time until now. But this morning—Lavender paused to tie the ribbons of her bonnet more firmly under her chin, for the wind was tugging the brim—she was aware of feeling decidedly out of sorts. In fact, she admitted to herself, it was worse than that. She felt blue-devilled.

Her mother, the Honourable Lavinia Brabant, had always maintained that a lady had no excuse for idleness or boredom. An informed and educated mind would always provide resources for solitude, and if that failed one should just remind oneself of the good fortune that had placed one in such an enviable position in life. Lavender felt very strongly that her mama had been quite right and would not approve of her daughter's current indisposition.

Lavender sighed. She knew that some of her restlessness sprang from the thoughts she had been having the previous day about her place at Hewly and her future plans. She felt unsettled, unfulfilled. Something was missing…

She went first to the church and laid some fresh flowers from the Hewly gardens on the grave of her father, Admiral Brabant. The graveside, in a quiet corner of the churchyard under a spreading oak, was peaceful and somehow comforting. Lavender sat down on a wooden seat nearby and rested her chin on her hand. Perhaps her father could help her sort her thoughts into some kind of order. He had always been a stickler for method and regulation during his lifetime.

It occurred to her that he had left her a considerable sum of money, and that that would enable her to leave Hewly if she so desired and to set up in a respectable house elsewhere. She could engage a companion—certainly she could afford to engage several—and if she were to find someone as amenable as Caroline, she would count herself lucky. Perhaps Lady Perceval could help her, for that matron was so well connected and well informed that she would know of any suitable persons seeking employment. The idea held some appeal but it also held some drawbacks. Lavender acknowledged that she liked living at Hewly and she liked the Abbey villages, and indeed, no one was trying to drive her away. Lewis and Caroline would no doubt be mortified if they even suspected her thoughts. She sighed again. Her musings did not seem to be getting her very far.

Lavender looked at the neat mound of her father's grave. She could imagine him addressing her, puffing out his chest in the imposing manner in which he used to lecture to his sailors: 'Action, not inaction is the solution to any crisis. Cease this foolish woolgathering, my girl, and get about your business!'

With a faint smile, Lavender got to her feet and picked up the basket.

She could always marry. The thought popped into her head as she was walking back around the church and heard the clock strike the hour. She had always been accustomed to thinking of herself as at her last prayers, but Caroline was nine and twenty, a good five years older than she. Perhaps there was a chance—although not much a chance of finding a husband as good as her brother.

Lavender considered the idea idly as she walked into the town. Her bridegroom would need to be an intelligent man who would appreciate a bluestocking wife and enjoy discussing weighty matters with her. He would encourage her sketching and her writing and would have plenty of interests of his own. He would not be at all the sort of man to want a pretty ninnyhammer, for she was well aware that her looks were no more than ordinary. He would need to be possessed of a reasonable competence, to live in the country and to shun the society pursuits that she had so detested when she had visited London. Lavender started to laugh at her own absurdity, but the thought persisted. As for age, well, she was prepared to accept an older man, for he was likely to have more sense, and as for looks... Here, with startling clarity, the face of Barnabas Hammond appeared before her eyes.

All Lavender's recent good humour vanished. She shook her head a little sharply to dispel the image but it was too late. She felt cross-grained and irritable and for two pins she would tell Caroline to run her own errands in future. She walked up the main street of Abbot Quincey positively scowling, and arrived in front of the draper's shop.

Hammonds General Store in Abbot Quincey was not as imposing as Arthur Hammond's emporium in Northampton, but it served a small town very well. Now that the seasons were turning, Mr Hammond had draped winter fustian and twilled cashmere about the door, and huge bolts of the cloth were stacked on shelves inside. Arthur Hammond himself was behind the counter and was encouraging the doctor's wife to feel the quality of the nankeen that he had spread out over the top. He was a big man, florid and full of bonhomie. As ever, he was smart in a tailed coat and old-fashioned knee breeches, with a waistcoat straining over his ample stomach. He always dressed like a gentleman.

'All our materials are purchased in London, of course,' Lavender heard him say, in the oily tone that she so detested, 'and you will not find a better quality of cloth anywhere, ma'am...'

He broke off when he saw Lavender and hurried to greet her, which set her teeth on edge even more. She noticed that Barney came forward unobtrusively from the shadows to smooth over his father's defection and flatter Mrs Pettifer into making the purchase. Lavender felt awkward. She had no wish for Hammond to snub the doctor's wife just because she was from Hewly Manor and Hammond always curried favour with his noble clients. Besides, she was only buying ribbons and thread.

Lavender's transaction was almost completed when Barney emerged from the stock-room carrying a trestle table obviously intended for the display of some new goods. He gave Lavender a slight nod as he passed, but did not even speak to her. She knew that he was working and did not have time for idle chatter, but nevertheless Lavender felt slightly crushed, and was annoyed with herself for feeling so.

She put her purse away, thanked Mr Hammond for his help, and made for the door.

It opened before she got there, to admit two girls whom Lavender recognised as the daughters of a farmer over towards Abbot Giles. Both had dark curly hair, and open, laughing faces. They were giggling together as they came into the shop, and edged over to the table where Barney was now arranging winter bonnets on the hat stands. Lavender paused to watch. Her first thought was how incongruous it was to see a man of Barney's calibre working on ladies bonnets. Her second thought was how much she disliked the giggling, pouting girls, who were now looking flirtatiously at Barney from under their lashes and asking him questions that were punctuated frequently by coy laughter.

As she stood in the doorway, Arthur Hammond bustled up, clearly unamused by all the banter. He berated Barney for his lack of skill with the display, cowed the girls with one sharp glance, and set to rearranging the bonnets, flitting here and there like a preening bird. It seemed to Lavender that whilst the son and heir had no disposition towards drapery, the father was obviously in his element. She went out into the street, wondering for the first time whether Mr Hammond found it frustrating that his eldest son had not inherited his talent as a merchant. She knew that Hammond was immensely successful, for as well as the emporium in Northampton he had a string of other shops in the county, and it was clearly his life's work. Barney, on the other hand, looked as though he would be much more at home in some other occupation.

She walked down the main street, past the bakery and the Angel inn. The sun was bright and Lavender had just decided to take her sketchbook out to do some drawing that afternoon, when there was a step behind her and a breathless voice called:

'Miss Brabant!'

She turned to see Ellen Hammond panting up the road behind her, face flushed with exertion. Hammond's daughter was about fifteen, and had inherited the dark looks that gave Barney his enigmatic air. Lavender thought that Ellen would probably be a beauty, but the girl showed no signs of being aware of it. She was smiling with unaffected pleasure.

'Oh, Miss Brabant, please excuse me! Barney— my brother—told me that you had given the kittens a good home and I so wished to thank you!'

Lavender smiled at her. 'I was happy to be of help, Miss Hammond! They are the most adorable creatures, are they not? You must come over to Hewly sometime and see how they progress!'

Ellen's face flushed pink. 'Oh! May I indeed? You are so kind, Miss Brabant!' Her expression crumpled. 'Father was going to drown them, you know! Of all the cruel things! But Barney is so kind and said that he would save them but that I was not to tell—'

'That's enough, Ellen. I am sure that Miss Brabant has other business to attend to in town!'

Neither of them had noticed Barney Hammond come round the side of the Angel inn. His hands were in his pockets and he looked relaxed enough, but his dark eyes were watchful. Ellen flushed at the implied rebuke and dropped a little curtsey. 'Excuse me, Miss Brabant,' she murmured. 'I did not intend to presume.'

Barney gave Lavender a slight bow and took his sister's arm. They turned away up the street together. Lavender, watching them go, was astonished to discover that she suddenly felt very angry. She was not sure if it was Barney Hammond's high-handed action in interrupting the conversation that had annoyed her, or the implication that Ellen should not push herself on her notice. Either way, she was not going to let the injustice pass.

'Mr Hammond!'

Barney and Ellen had only gone five paces and both stopped at the imperious tone. Anxious not to add to the impression of upper-class hauteur, Lavender added politely: 'Mr Hammond. I should like to speak to you, if you please!'

She saw Barney hesitate, before he bent and spoke softly to Ellen and the girl scooted off up the road on her own. Barney turned back to Lavender and came forward courteously. His expression showed nothing but polite enquiry, but Lavender wondered what he was thinking behind that inscrutable façade.

'Miss Brabant?'

Lavender was feeling nervous. She cleared her throat and fixed him with a stern look. 'Mr Hammond, there was no need to reprimand your sister. She was doing no harm. She is a charming girl.'

Barney's civil expression did not waver. He met her look with an equally straight one of his own.

'Miss Brabant, I am sure that you mean well, but I do beg you not to encourage Ellen. Your kind attentions would be sufficient to turn her head, and that would only lead her to wish for more than she could have.'

There was a long moment whilst their eyes met and held and Lavender had the strangest feeling that he was not simply referring to Ellen's situation. Her eyes narrowed in a frown, but before she could speak, Barney had sketched a bow and walked away.

Lavender's heart was thudding. She watched his tall figure catch Ellen up, saw them exchange a few words, then Barney took her hand and together they strolled up the road, swinging their linked hands as they walked. Lavender felt the foolish tears prickle her eyes. She need scarcely have worried that Ellen would have been hurt by Barney's reproach. The sign of family unity contradicted that firmly. She was the one left feeling heart-sore. There was no doubt that she had been warned off, and for a misplaced act of kindness too. Yet she could not help but believe that there was more to it than that.

Lavender burned with embarrassment to think that Barney might have been addressing his words directly to her. Suppose he imagined that she was developing some sort of *tendre* for him and was trying to advise her that her feelings were inappropriate. It was true that she had imagined that there was some warmth in his manner towards her and had liked it. And last night, when they had met in the wood… A wave of mortification swept over her as she remembered how distracted she had been by the warmth of his touch and the hardness of his body against hers. She was glowering fiercely by the time she reached the end of the street. She had liked and admired Barney Hammond, she told herself angrily, but that was entirely at an end. She doubted that she would ever speak to him again.

Lavender had always found sketching to be soothing for a troubled mind. During her father's last illness she had derived great comfort from her drawing, and had even tentatively started work on a pictorial catalogue of the flora of the Steepwood Abbey woodlands. She was meticulously accurate in her sketches and thought that the work had some merit, although she did not dare hope that it would be good enough for publication. Now, however, her work offered just the solace that Lavender needed, and after luncheon she set off with her sketchbook and crayons, and went into the forest.

It was a beautiful day. The sunlight ran in dappled rivulets beneath the trees and the canopy was alive with the sound of birds, the loud laughing call of the green woodpecker and the chatter of the jay. The leaves were starting to fall and were crunchy beneath her feet and between their crisp covering the mushrooms pushed up. She spread her rug on a bank and sketched a few of the most colourful ones: the amethyst deceiver, with its vivid violet blue cap, and the verdigris toadstool that nestled in the grassy clearings. Gradually the fresh air and the peace had their desired effect and Lavender started to feel better. She drew a clump of wood vetch whose tendrils were clamped around a nearby tree stump. She knelt down to fix the detail of the purple-veined flowers and the fat, black seed pods, and it was only when she got up again that she saw that her skirt was streaked with earth and green with grass stains. The sun was lower now and she knew she had been out for several hours. She studied the sketch; it was good, the proportions were correct and the detail accurate, and she was happy to add it to her portfolio. Perhaps she would even show Caroline what she had done, for her sister-in-law was a keen amateur botanist.

Lavender packed up her bag, dusted her skirt down, and fixed her bonnet more securely on her head, retying the ribbons. Her hair was coming down and escaping from under the bonnet's brim—long, straight strands of very fine fair hair that got caught on the breeze. Her cousin Julia had told her often that she was plain and Lavender knew that it was true that she seldom took care of her appearance, but just lately she had thought that her deep blue eyes were a little bit pretty and her figure quite good… Finding by some strange coincidence that her thoughts were drifting from her own appearance to that of Barnabas Hammond, Lavender hastily started to plan the next drawing for her catalogue.

She was walking along, weighing the rival merits of Caper Spurge and Mountain Melick Grass—neither of them colourful, but both an important part of the botanical record—when she heard the strangest sound and paused to listen. It was not a woodland noise at all—not a sound with which she was very familiar and certainly not one she expected to hear in Steepwood. It was the unmistakable sound of steel on steel.

Edging forward, Lavender crept down a path that was closely bordered by scrub and the pressing trees. It was not a path she had taken before, but she knew she was walking in the direction of Steepwood Lawn and was not afraid she would become lost. She was more afraid of being seen, but curiosity held her in a strong grip and she picked her way silently and with care. Within a hundred yards the forest fell back, revealing a sweep of green turf that was ideal for a duel and it was here that the contest was taking place. Lavender crept as close as she dared, staying in the cover of the trees. She took refuge behind one broad trunk and peeped round.

She had seen very few fencing matches, for it was not an activity of which most gently bred females had much experience. Years before, Lewis and Andrew had staged mock fights in the courtyard at Hewly, but Andrew was always too indolent to take them seriously and Lewis had won very quickly. Lavender could tell that this was no such match. She knew that the two men fighting here were doing so for pleasure rather than in earnest, for she could see the buttons on their foils, but she could also tell that they were taking it very seriously. Both were skilled swordsmen and fought with strength and determination, giving no quarter.

Lavender leant a little closer. One of the men was a complete stranger to her, a fair-haired giant who moved more slowly than his opponent but had the benefit of strength and reach. The other was only a few inches shorter, dark, lithe, muscular... Lavender gave a little squeak and clapped her hand over her mouth. There was no mistake—it had to be Barnabas Hammond.

It was fortunate that the noise of the contest drowned out Lavender's involuntary gasp, for the last thing that she wanted was to be discovered. She stood, both hands pressed against the tree trunk, and stared. A ridiculous image of Barney as she had seen him that very morning floated before her eyes, a vision of him arranging hats on a trestle table. It was absurd. That man and this could surely not be the same—yet when the movement of the fight brought him round so that she could see his face again, Lavender knew there could be no mistake. Forgetting concealment, she simply stood and watched.

He moved with a speed and strength that held Lavender spellbound. There was something utterly compelling about his confidence and skill. Her avid gaze took in the way his sweat-damp shirt clung to the lines of his shoulders and back, and moved on with mesmerised attention to his close-fitting buckskins and bare feet. His shirt was open at the throat, revealing the strong, brown column of his neck, and the sun glinted on the tawny strands in his hair and turned his skin to a deep bronze. When he finally succeeded in disarming his opponent with a move that sent the other man's foil flying through the air, he threw back his head and laughed.

'A fine match! You get better, James, I swear you do!'

Lavender watched as the fair man retrieved his foil from the bushes and threw himself down on the grass. He was laughing too. 'I rue the day I ever crossed swords with you, Barney! I would challenge you to another round for my revenge, but I am prom-

ised to a party at Jaffrey House and dare not be late!'
He sat up, grinning, and started to pull on his boots.
'You do not know how fortunate you are to be spared
such things, old fellow! If it were not for the beautiful blue eyes of a certain Miss Sheldon, I doubt I
could stomach it!' He sighed. 'But she is the most
angelic creature...'

'Spare me.' Lavender saw Barney grin. 'Last time
I saw you, it was a certain Lady Georgiana Cutler
who had taken your fancy!'

'I know!' The fair-haired man got to his feet. He
shook his head. 'I am fickle! But Lady Georgiana
could not hold a candle to Miss Sheldon—'

'Take your languishings off elsewhere,' Barney
advised, picking up his foil. 'I shall take me to the
shop and work at my books whilst you are carous-
ing!'

'Life is damnably unfair!' The other man grinned,
clapping him on the back. 'You to your studies and
me to my fortune-hunting! Ah well. I'll see you in
Northampton, no doubt.'

They shook hands and Lavender watched him
walk off in the direction of Jaffrey House, both foils
tucked under his arm. She stayed quite still, watching, as Barney pulled his boots on and started to walk
slowly across the greensward towards the trees. His
head was bent and the dark hair had fallen across his
forehead. He smoothed it back with an absent-

minded gesture. Lavender could hear him whistling under his breath, a lilting tune that hung on the air.

She froze where she stood as he passed close by. Of all the odd things she had seen in Steepwood, this had to be amongst the strangest. That Barney Hammond should be such a superlative swordsman was extraordinary, since she could not imagine that fencing was amongst the pursuits that he had learned as a boy. Then there was his friendship with a gentleman who was clearly staying at Jaffrey House, the home of the Earl of Yardley. Lavender had heard that a party was staying at the house and if the Brabants had not been in mourning, they would have been invited to join them. She frowned. It was very odd. But perhaps she was simply being snobbish—again—in expecting Barney to conform to her expectations. He really was a most mysterious man…

At that moment, craning to get a last glimpse of him before he entered the trees, Lavender took a step forward. There was a deafening snap by her left ankle, something tugged hard at her skirts, and she tumbled over in the grass. The tree canopy spun above her head and her bonnet went bouncing away across the clearing, leaving her sprawled in a heap with her petticoats around her knees and a sharp pain in her left leg. She sat up a little unsteadily and bent to inspect the damage.

There was a rusty iron trap snapped shut around her skirts, its teeth grinning at her in an evil parody of a smile. Lavender felt a little faint as she realised how close she had come to stepping on it. Another few inches and it would have been her leg between those metal jaws, her bones broken without a doubt. She had seen traps before, man-traps and spring-guns and leg-breakers like this one set to catch poachers, but she had had no idea that she might stumble on such a thing in Steep Wood. She could not imagine who would have set such a trap.

Worse was to come. From her position prone in the grass she could no longer see Barney, but it seemed impossible that he had not heard the trap going off or the alarm call of the birds as they scattered into the tops of the trees at the sudden noise. Panicking, Lavender tried to get to her feet, then sat down again in a hurry when the weight of the trap made her over-balance. She could not prise it open and it was too heavy for her to pick up, though she would definitely have made a run for it, trap and all, if she could have done so. She could now hear footsteps, coming closer, and she knew they had to belong to Barney. She closed her eyes in an agony of mortification.

There was a step in the grass beside her, then Barney's voice said, 'Miss Brabant! What in God's name—'

Lavender opened her eyes. The wind was ruffling his thick dark hair as he stared down at her from what seemed a great height. He had a casual shooting jacket slung over his shoulder, and at close quarters she could see that his buckskins fitted like a second skin and his shirt was still clinging to his muscular torso. Feeling hot and very peculiar, Lavender closed her eyes again.

She was not sure what was the most embarrassing aspect of her current situation. Perhaps it was being found in such an undignified tumble by such an attractive man, or perhaps the fact that he would guess she had been spying on him was even more embarrassing. She kept her eyes closed and hoped he would go away.

He did not. Lavender reluctantly opened her eyes again.

She saw his gaze go to the cut in her leg, and tweaked her skirts down as best she could, but not before he had seen the tell-tale trickle of blood. He frowned and went down on one knee beside her in the grass.

'You are injured! Have you fallen and hurt yourself—'

The trap was all but covered by Lavender's skirts. She gestured towards it. 'As you can see, sir, I have had an accident.'

Barney's gaze went from her reddening face to the rusty trap. He bit his lip. Lavender would have sworn that he was about to laugh.

'Oh dear. I see. Presumably it is too heavy for you to hobble home?'

Lavender's face reddened even more, this time with fury. 'Your amusement is misplaced, sir! It is not remotely funny that people go around setting traps strong enough to break a man's leg! If you cannot find anything more constructive to say, perhaps you should leave me to deal with it as best I may!'

'I'm sorry.' Barney spoke gently. 'Take comfort from the fact that it did not in fact break any bones. Although,' his gaze turned back to her ankle, which Lavender was trying to hide under her skirts, 'I did think that you had sustained a graze…'

'It is nothing!' Lavender snapped. She did not think that she was spoilt but she felt she was entitled to feel a little sorry for herself. The refusal of this man to sympathise with her predicament was infuriating. Barney was still kneeling by her side and she wished that he would just go away.

'My sister Ellen was caught in a man-trap in these woods once,' he said conversationally. 'She was not as fortunate as you, Miss Brabant. She fell into the pit and pierced her arm on a spike. She bears the scar to this day.'

Lavender was silenced. Suddenly the tears of shock and self-pity were not far away. She sniffed and turned her head away so that he would not see.

'I am sorry,' she said, a little stiffly, 'but who would do such a thing—'

'The Marquis of Sywell, I imagine.' Barney had

picked up the trap and was attempting unsuccessfully to open it. 'He used to derive much pleasure from maiming and killing—man or beast, it did not matter. This is an old trap of his, I am sure.' He looked at her. 'I am sorry, but I cannot move it. You will have to take off your skirt.'

He spoke in such a matter-of-fact tone that at first Lavender did not register the sense of his words. Then she did and forgot her tears in her outrage. She glared at him. 'How can you be so nonsensical, Mr Hammond! I shall do no such thing!'

Barney grinned. 'Come now, Miss Brabant, this is no time to be missish! I had thought you had more sense than most ladies of your class, but it seems I was wrong!' He stood up. 'Have no concern for my feelings! I have three sisters and shall not be shocked!'

Lavender stared, open-mouthed. It had not occurred to her that he was about to watch.

'But Mr Hammond, you must go away!'

'Miss Brabant,' Barney gave her a quizzical smile, 'if I am to help you, I must stay.'

Lavender tried to struggle to her feet and stumbled as the weight of the trap bore her down again. Immediately, Barney's arm was about her waist. She could feel the warmth of his hand through the cotton of her dress.

'Let me assist you—'

'No!' Lavender almost yelped with fright at his touch. 'Go away! I can manage perfectly well!'

She realised that she did indeed sound like one of the hen-witted society girls that she so despised. Barney was laughing at her, a twinkle deep in those dark eyes.

'If I let you go you will fall over. Now, pray be sensible, Miss Brabant. You will either need to remove the skirt or at the very least, rip off the offending piece—'

'Thank you,' Lavender said, knowing that she sounded sulky. 'I had worked that out for myself! If you will stand a little off, Mr Hammond, I shall do what is necessary!'

Barney gave her another grin and let her go very gently. Once Lavender had found her balance she discovered that she could manage perfectly well, and was even able to hop into the shelter of a nearby oak, dragging the trap behind her. Having checked suspiciously that Barney was being as good as his word and had turned his back, she slipped her skirt off, her fingers clumsy in their haste. Once she was free of it, it was a relatively simple matter to tear off the strip that was caught, and rearrange the rest about her as decently as possible. When she had finished, she decided that she looked almost respectable, if a little odd. The left-hand side of the skirt was a little lop-sided at the hem, showing a couple of inches of petticoat and an entirely improper glimpse of ankle, but it could have been so much worse. Her leg was sore and stiff from the cut, but she was tolerably certain that she could manage to limp home.

Barney was whistling again, the lilting tune that she had heard earlier. As she came out of the shade of the trees he turned to look at her, and Lavender's heart did a little skip at his long, slow scrutiny.

'Can you manage to walk home, Miss Brabant, or shall I carry you?' he asked. 'I saw that you had a nasty cut to your leg.'

'I can manage, I thank you,' Lavender said, feeling quite weak at the thought of Barney picking her up in his arms.

'Then I shall carry your bag rather than your person,' Barney said, stooping to pick up the bag with Lavender's sketches and crayons. 'I should not like to outrage your sensibilities any further.'

'There is no need to accompany me at all,' Lavender argued, her temper decidedly scratchy by now. 'And whilst we are settling our differences, Mr Hammond, I must ask you not to make patronising assumptions about me! I am no feather-brained girl to fall into a swoon just because I have a small accident! If it comes to that, *you* are very different inside your father's shop from out of it, but you do not hear me making ill-bred observations!'

There was a taut silence, but for a wood pigeon cooing in the branches above their heads. Then Barney gave a slight nod. His gaze was very steady.

'Very well, Miss Brabant. I accept your reproof—
if you will accept my escort back home.'

Lavender shrugged with an ill grace. She went
ahead of him to the path, trying not to limp too obviously as she struggled with brambles and the grasping stems of dog rose that seemed determined to rip
the rest of her skirt from her. She was beginning to
wish that she had never let curiosity get the better of
her when she had heard the fencing match.

Pride could only get her so far. Eventually they
came to a place where a fallen tree had blocked the
path, and she was obliged to accept Barney's hand
to help her over it. After that he walked by her side,
kicking a stray branch from her path and holding
back the straggling stems of rose and bindweed
whenever they threatened to catch on her clothes.
Lavender tried to repress the treacherous feeling of
warmth that this engendered, but it was impossible
not to feel more in charity with him for such gallantry. Then, when they had been walking in silence
for about five minutes, he said, 'I infer from your
remark about my being a different person outside the
shop that you saw the fencing match, Miss Brabant?'

Lavender stole a quick look at his face and
blushed.

'I am sorry… It is not that I was watching, but the
noise of the contest attracted my notice and I stopped
to see what was happening—'

'I see.' She thought Barney sounded as though he saw rather too much. 'No doubt you were surprised?'

'Well, I…' Lavender struggled to think of a way of expressing her feelings without sounding rude. 'I suppose I was. It was not something that I expected you…' She broke off. 'That is, you seemed very proficient—' She stopped again. Now she had given away that she had been watching long enough to make a judgement.

'Thank you.' Barney was smiling at her. 'No doubt it must seem odd to you, but I have been fencing since I was a boy. James Oliver, my opponent a few moments back, was also my first adversary. I met him and a few of his aristocratic playmates when I was about eleven, and walking in the forest.' He shot her a look. 'They taunted me, the poor village boy, and I was so angry that I challenged James to a fight. Imagine my dismay when he suggested we should fight with swords, like gentlemen rather than peasants, as he put it!'

Lavender could not help smiling at his droll tone. 'What happened?'

The laughter lines around Barney's eyes deepened. 'Well, no doubt I was a little unorthodox in my style, but I discovered that I had a natural bent for fencing! I beat James easily and then he and his friends did not crow so loud! And since then he has sworn he will beat me one day, but he has yet to do so!'

'He seems a better friend to you now than he must

have been then,' Lavender ventured, for one of the things that had struck her about the two men was their easy camaraderie.

Barney laughed. 'Oh, he learned respect! No, James is a good fellow at heart and I have counted him a friend for many years now.' He hesitated. 'All the same, Miss Brabant, I should be grateful if you told no one that you witnessed our match.'

Lavender stopped, taken aback. 'Of course, if you wish it! But is this some strange kind of reverse snobbery that prompts you not to acknowledge your aristocratic friends, Mr Hammond?'

She could have bitten her tongue out as soon as she had spoken, for she knew she did not know him well enough to ask such a personal and challenging question. Whilst Lavender had little time for the commonplaces and evasions of polite society, she did at least feel that she always spoke with courtesy. This time, however, she had been lured by the unusual nature of their conversation into asking a rather direct question. She saw Barney raise his eyebrows at her plain speaking, but he did not seem in any way taken aback and he answered her without prevarication.

'Not at all. The truth is that I prefer not to tell anyone. Were my father to know I fear he would take shameless advantage.'

Lavender turned aside and started walking again. She felt a little embarrassed. She knew exactly what he meant. Arthur Hammond was such a social climber that he would be beside himself with excitement to discover that Barney had such upper-class friends. No doubt he would use the fact to push himself on their notice and ruin the comfortable companionship that existed.

'Have you kept it a secret for all these years, then?' she asked, unable to prevent her curiosity surfacing again.

'Oh, it is but one of many secrets!' Barney said easily. Lavender saw a hint of amusement in his eyes as he watched her. 'In general terms, Miss Brabant, I find it easier not to tell people things!'

Lavender struggled to equate this with what she thought she knew of him. It was true that most of it had been based on assumption and conjecture, about the shop, about his father, about his life... Just as he had apparently seen her as a spoilt society miss, she had imagined him to be the son of a solid merchant family, destined inevitably to take over the business one day. Now, suddenly, all her ideas were in a spin.

They had reached the stile at the edge of the wood and paused whilst still under the shadows of the trees. The sun was slanting through the leaves in blinding shafts. Lavender put up a hand to shade her eyes.

'Thank you for carrying my portfolio. I am sure I can manage from here back to Hewly—'

'At the least, let me help you over the stile,' Barney murmured. Before Lavender could either ac-

cept or decline, he had swept her up in his arms and
deposited her on the other side, ruffled and indignant.
She grabbed hold of him to steady herself. The material of his shirt was soft beneath her fingers and
once again, Lavender could feel the warmth and the
hardness of the muscle beneath. She positively
jumped away from him.

'Really, sir—'

'Miss Brabant? Surely you did not wish to risk
further injury to your ankle?'

Barney handed her the portfolio. 'Will you show
me your drawings one day? I should be most interested…'

Lavender looked at him suspiciously but he
seemed quite in earnest. 'If you would truly care to
see them—'

Barney flashed her a smile. 'Thank you. I will
leave you here, Miss Brabant, if you are sure that
you can manage alone. And take care when you are
walking in the forest. You can never be sure what
you might find.'

Lavender felt the colour come into her cheeks
again. His gaze was very steady and in a second,
mortification overcame her. He had made no direct
reference to her spying on the fencing match that
afternoon, but suddenly her guilty conscience was
too much and she was sure that he *knew*—knew that
it was not the first time she had watched him. Some
two months previously she had been wandering

through the woods where the river ran, and had seen Barney in the pool beneath the trees. He had been swimming strongly and the water had streamed over his bare brown shoulders and down his back, and Lavender had wanted to strip down to her shift and join him in the water there and then… A huge wash of guilty colour swept into her face, and she turned and ran from him, regardless of her torn skirt, the pain in her leg, and the amazed expression she knew must be on his face as he watched her run away.

Chapter Three

'Lavender, you have had a Friday face for at least the past week!' Caroline observed to her sister-in-law, ten days later. 'I declare, you are making me miserable, and I was in the greatest good spirits until this morning! Whatever can be the matter with you?'

Lavender refused to look up from her book. She did not want to face Caroline's shrewd questioning at the moment. They were sitting in the drawing-room, Caroline embroidering and Lavender half-heartedly reading *Sense and Sensibility*. She was dismally aware that she was not enjoying herself—and had not done so ever since her disastrous encounter with Barney Hammond in the wood.

The scratch on her leg had healed quickly, but her feelings were still sore. She was uncomfortably aware that she had made a complete cake of herself. It had been undignified enough to have been caught in the man-trap but she had made matters infinitely worse for herself by running away in so melodramatic a fashion.

'It is nothing of consequence,' she muttered, knowing she sounded ungracious. 'I am sorry if my poor spirits are lowering to yours. I shall go into the library.'

She made to get up, but Caroline put out a hand to stay her.

'Do not sulk! I was only teasing.' She patted the sofa beside her and Lavender sat down reluctantly. 'In fact I have the best of news! You know that Lewis is to go to Northampton on business for a few days?'

Lavender nodded.

'Well, by great good chance I have just had a letter from Lady Anne Covingham this morning. The family are at Riding Park for a se'nnight from Friday, and urge us to join them. It will be the very thing! We may stay at the Park and visit in Northampton, and be as merry as grigs!'

Lavender fidgeted uneasily. 'I am not sure,' she said doubtfully. 'I do not feel inclined for company at the moment, Caro—'

Caroline opened her eyes wide. 'Upon my word, you are very retiring at present! I know you did not enjoy your London Season, but you are perfectly at ease in good company and the Covinghams are not so high in the instep to put one in dislike! Why, they have always treated me with friendship even when I worked for them!' Her face changed. 'But I shall not force you to go if you do not wish it. If you will not be comfortable, dearest Lavender, you must stay here—'

Lavender shook her head. The thought of staying at Hewly on her own seemed even worse than that of going away. Impatient with herself, she smiled at her sister-in-law.

'I'm sorry, Caro. Take no notice of me, I am in a fit of the megrims at the moment! A change of scene is just what I need.'

'Capital!' Caroline smiled. 'I shall write to Anne directly. You will see, Lavender—it shall be just the thing!'

Their first evening at Riding Park was a comfortable one. The house party was small and consisted only of themselves, Lady Anne Covingham and her husband Lord Freddie, and the youngest Covingham daughter, Frances. Frances was eighteen and a lively brunette, and Lavender eyed her with caution. She had met girls like Frances Covingham during her London Season, and was miserably aware that she had nothing in common with them.

Lady Anne was exactly as Caroline had promised. Small, dark and vivacious, she possessed a warmth of manner that immediately made Lavender feel at home. Lord Freddie was equally charming and they all seemed utterly delighted to see Caroline again, and to get to know her new family. Miss Covingham in particular was thrilled to see her old governess and fell on Caroline's neck with tears of joy.

They dined *en famille* the first night, with no ostentatious display of plate or silver, though Lady Anne was at pains to explain that this was not out of a lack of respect for their visitors, but simply because they considered Caroline so much a part of the family. She explained that there was to be a dinner and ball in a few days, but in the meantime they preferred the house party to be informal. As though to underline this fact, the gentlemen did not linger over their port, but rejoined the ladies quickly for tea in the drawing-room, where Miss Covingham played a number of Schubert pieces. She performed prettily and with competence and Lavender, who had never been musical, felt her fragile spirits sink again. She was glad that no one asked her to play, for after Frances's skill she knew she would have sounded like an elephant clattering over the keys.

When Frances had finished, she came over to the window-seat and sat down next to Lavender with a smile. Lavender smiled back, a little hesitantly.

'You play very well, Miss Covingham! You must have a natural talent for music!'

Frances laughed, her big brown eyes sparkling. 'Truth to tell,' she confided, 'the credit for my playing should go to Miss Whiston—Mrs Brabant, that is. I was a terrible pupil and though I shall never be truly talented, Mrs Brabant persisted until I was at least no embarrassment!' She smiled across at Caroline, who was deep in conversation with Lady Anne. 'Oh, it was a sad day for me when Miss Whiston left us, for she was the greatest good friend to us all!'

'You must have missed her a lot,' Lavender ventured.

Frances gave her a dazzling smile. 'Oh, prodigiously! My two sisters were already married, you see, and I was very lonely! But we always fought over who should have Miss Whiston, for we were all most attached to her! When she married, my sister Louisa wanted Miss Whiston to go with her as her companion, you know, but Harriet and I could not bear to spare her! And Miss Whiston said that it would be better for Louisa and Cheverton to have some time on their own.' She frowned. 'Louisa is volatile, you know, and she and Cheverton were forever arguing! But they rub along tolerably well together now and have two delightful babies, so I suppose they must have settled their differences!'

Lavender blinked slightly at this insight into the Cheverton marriage. 'And your other sister, Miss Covingham—Harriet, is it? You said that she is married as well?'

Her sisters' marriages were evidently a perennially interesting topic with Frances, who wriggled slightly on the window-seat as she settled down for a really good gossip.

'Oh yes, Miss Brabant, Harriet is married to Lord John Farley—Stapleton's heir, you know. But I fear they do not suit.' Her round face took on a doleful expression. She leaned closer to Lavender and dropped her voice to a whisper. 'Mama and Papa were not at all happy about the match, you know, but Harri is headstrong and threatened to elope! Well, she nearly set the house by the ears! Mama was in a fit of the vapours and Papa was storming around and threatening to horsewhip the fellow, until Miss Whiston made everyone calm. She spoke to Harriet, you know, but she could not persuade her! I was listening at the door, and heard Miss Whiston— Mrs Brabant—tell Harri that Farley was a womaniser who would make her unhappy, but Harri was hot for him and would not listen!' Frances shrugged her plump white shoulders philosophically. 'So in the end Papa gave his consent and they were married and now,' she dropped her voice confidentially, 'he keeps a mistress quite openly and Harri is as miserable as sin!'

She sat back and opened her eyes very wide. 'Now what do you think of that, Miss Brabant!'

'I am sorry for your sister,' Lavender said truthfully. 'It must be a dreadful thing to love a man who does not care as much for you.'

'Oh, Harri fancied herself in love with him,'

Frances said, assuming a world-weary air that seemed far in advance of her years, 'but it was all a nonsense! Why, now she has a *tendre* for another gentleman, and is thinking of running off with him—' She broke off, seeing that both Caroline and her mother were eavesdropping, and bit her lip. 'Anyway, I should not gossip so! But Harri has caused me no end of trouble,' she added gloomily, 'because I was to have my come-out this year, but with all the fuss over Harri's wedding, Mama thought it best to wait until I was older and more sensible! She says that the three of us are headstrong and flighty but I would never be so foolish!'

Lavender laughed. She was finding it impossible to dislike Frances Covingham. On the one hand she epitomised everything that Lavender had always thought she had an aversion to in young ladies. She was dark and modish, and had no interest in scholarship and a fascination with fashion and gossip that Lavender found quite tedious. On the other hand, she was clearly a sweet-natured girl and Caroline had obviously worked hard to instil in her a set of values that went beyond the money and consequence granted by her position. Lavender realised that Frances's uncomplicated warmth and friendliness were a far cry from the haughty snobbery that she had encountered during her London Season.

Frances smoothed her skirts. 'Forgive me, Miss Brabant. I am such a sad rattle! Tell me about yourself, and about Hewly Manor. It sounds a delightful place…'

'Oh, I am a poor subject of conversation,' Lavender said hastily, 'but I am always happy to talk of Hewly! It is a beautiful house and I love to wander in the grounds and the countryside—'

'By yourself?' Frances looked struck halfway between incredulity and respect. 'Only fancy!'

'Oh yes, for there is no danger in the woods and lanes—'

Lavender broke off, remembering that sometimes one met with the unexpected in Steep Wood.

'Fancy!' Miss Covingham repeated vaguely. 'Indeed, it sounds delightfully pastoral!' Her brow wrinkled. 'You will be sorry to leave Hewly when you marry then, Miss Brabant!'

Lavender frowned slightly at what seemed to be a *non sequitur*. 'Oh! But there is no likelihood of that, Miss Covingham! I am well past my last prayers and do not intend to marry!'

It seemed she had uttered the unthinkable. Frances gave a little shriek and caught her arm. 'Oh, Miss Brabant!' Frances said breathlessly. 'But that is impossible! Of course you must marry!'

Lavender raised her eyebrows, smiling. 'Indeed! Must I? Why so, Miss Covingham?'

'Well…' Frances seemed quite taken aback at the challenge. Lavender waited confidently for her to say that all girls should hunt themselves a husband, but when Frances finally replied it literally took Lavender's breath away.

'Because you are so pretty!' her new-found friend declared triumphantly. 'Oh Miss Brabant, it would be such a waste otherwise!'

Later, when Frances had said goodnight with many professions of friendship and had promised to show her the estate the following day, Lavender lay in her vast bed and looked up at the scarlet drapes that hung above her head. It was foolish for a woman of sense to be so moved by a compliment, and yet when Frances had declared how pretty she was, Lavender had almost asked her if she was sure. Perhaps it was true. Her hair was, after all, a very attractive silver gilt colour—not the fashionable golden blonde of the London beauties, perhaps, but still quite nice. And she had often been told that her deep lavender blue eyes were her best feature… Smiling slightly, she fell asleep and dreamed, rather improbably, of ribbons and lace, and gowns of rose crêpe and lavender to match her eyes.

The following day was fair and whilst Lewis went off into Northampton to see his man of business, the ladies took a carriage and drove about the estate. Riding Park was a very fine house, an Elizabethan mansion in red brick, with rolling parkland and a beautiful lake. Lavender was particularly taken with the hunting-lodge, which stood between the walled gardens and the park, and Frances gleefully told her that it was haunted by the ghost of the first owner, Sir Thomas Gleason, who was supposed to walk from the Lodge to the house on stormy nights.

'They say he was a philanthropist who bemoans the fact that the money he left in trust for the poor was stolen by the rich,' Frances confided, her eyes huge. 'He walks with his steeple hat under one arm, and wears a ruff, doublet and hose! What do you think of that, Miss Brabant! I declare I should faint with fright were I to see him!'

'They do say that Hewly is haunted,' Caroline put in, from her seat opposite the girls. 'The Grey Lady, is it not, Lavender? I have never seen her, but they say she stalks the house when there is about to be a death in the family.'

Frances shivered enjoyably. 'Oh, how Gothic! Poor, desperate creature that she must be!'

Caroline and Lavender exchanged a smile.

'Frances is the dearest creature, is she not?' Caroline said later, when, having dressed for dinner she came along to see how Lavender was progressing. 'I was so hoping that the two of you would be friends. For although you have scarcely an interest in common, I dare swear you think her the sweetest girl!'

Lavender was spending longer in front of the mirror than was customary, for she was trying out a new

hairstyle, one that involved a bandeau of pale green
to match her dress. It also entailed a complicated
procedure of curling her hair into ringlets and gathering them up on one side of her head. The suggestion had quite taken her maid by surprise and con-
sequently had thrown her into a fluster until Caroline
had appeared and had the good sense to call
Frances's own maid to help. The result was rather
pleasing, Lavender thought, as she turned this way
and that to admire her reflection.

'Oh, Frances is a lovely girl,' she agreed heartily,
gathering up her bag and fan. 'She has promised to
help me dress for the ball on Friday night. And we
are to go shopping together in Northampton tomorrow, Caro. Is this not fun!'

And she totally failed to see Caroline's expression
of amused surprise as she swept out of the room on
the way down to dinner.

The whole party drove into Northampton on the
following day. Although Lavender had been to the
town several times before, this was the first time that
she had approached from the west, over the river and
up Black Lion Hill into the Marefair. As they grew
near, the whole town was spread out before them and
they all agreed it to be a very fine sight indeed. On
such a sunny day the jumble of roofs shone in the
light and the stone gleamed warm.

They drove past St Peter's Church, and into the

Horsemarket, and Lady Anne requested that the coach set them down in Mercers Row.

Lavender leant forward to look at the passing shops and houses. 'The buildings are very fine, are they not? I do so wish I could come into the town again just to walk round and admire the architecture! A sight-seeing tour of the churches would be great fun, for I know I have read that they are all very splendid…'

Frances, who had been discussing with her mother the rival merits of several dressmakers' shops, broke off, looking horrified. 'A tour of the churches…' She caught Lady Anne's eye and recovered herself. 'Well, if you wish it, dearest Lavender, I shall be happy to accompany you.'

Lavender smiled at her. 'You are very noble, Frances, but I should not put you to so much trouble! I know that ancient monuments are not to everyone's taste!'

Frances looked relieved. 'Well, I'll own that it is not a great interest of mine, but I do assure you, Lavender, that I should be very pleased to go with you!' She brightened. 'Indeed, I could act as guide myself! I remember that St Sepulchre's church is one of a very few in the country with a round tower.' She screwed her face up. 'It dates from the…thirteenth century! There! Mrs Brabant! Are you not proud of me!' And she dissolved into irre- sistible giggles at the looks of frank amazement on everyone's faces. 'Oh dear, I shall never be a bluestocking, but I can still surprise you all!'

They dismounted from the carriage at the Bear inn, and swiftly went their separate ways. Lord Freddie wanted to visit the gunsmith's and Lewis arranged to meet him there after he had consulted his man of business. Meanwhile Frances and Lady Anne needed to call in at the drapers to pick a few final necessities for the ball. Frances also wanted to visit the milliners, the haberdashers, the linen-drapers and the perfumiers, but Lady Anne shook her head decisively over this last and said that *poudre subtil* was not appropriate for young girls. Frances was not squashed and caught Lavender's arm, eagerly encouraging her to look in the window of the first of many drapers' shops.

'Oh Lavender, look at that bonnet! Now which would be most becoming, the red or the green?'

Lavender looked at her thoughtfully. 'I do believe the green would suit your colouring best, Frances. The red is pretty, but the green matches your eyes.'

Frances seemed much struck by this. 'I do believe you are right, Lavender! You have good taste! Well, we shall see!' She rummaged in her reticule. 'I fear I have little of my allowance left, but there may be just enough… But I will not choose just yet, for there are so many other shops to see!'

Lavender, who had not intended making any purchases, found that under Frances's encouragement it

was easy to buy a very pretty spencer tippet and a
fur muff for winter. She watched with amusement as
Frances swept through each shop, collecting ostrich
feathers, silk gloves and embroidered handkerchiefs
with complete abandonment. Finally, when Frances
had declared her interest in a Turkish turban,
Lavender was forced to intervene and point out that
it made her look too matronly.

'I do not know how you may be so sparing,
Lavender,' Frances complained, looking from her
own pile of purchases to Lavender's modest parcel.
'Why, you should be stocking up with all the nec-
essaries for a tolerable winter! Surely the best shops
in Abbot Quincey cannot match your choice here!'

Lavender turned away and pretended to examine
a blue scarf. 'We have the best draper's imaginable
in Abbot's Quincey,' she said lightly. 'Arthur
Hammond himself—'

'Hammonds!' Frances squeaked excitedly. 'I had
all but forgot! We cannot go back without a visit to
his emporium!'

Lavender hung back, suddenly wishing she had
not been prompted to mention the name. She did not
wish to risk a visit to Arthur Hammond's shop, although it was scarcely likely that Barney would be
there.

'But we have plenty of purchases already,
Frances!' she said hastily. 'You will be bankrupting
yourself with any more!'

Frances brushed this aside. 'What nonsense!' She hurried across to the counter, where Lady Anne was buying some embroidered muslin. 'Mama, I know we are due back any moment, but may we just call in at Hammonds on the way? Oh please… They have the very best goods…'

The shop assistant serving Lady Anne gave Frances a glare at the mention of such a rival, but Lady Anne seemed nothing loath.

'Very well, my love,' she said, 'but only for a moment or the gentlemen will set off home without us!'

Lavender made her way over to Caroline, who was resting on a chair in an alcove whilst she waited for the others.

'Does it suit you to go on to another shop, dearest Caro?' Lavender asked anxiously. 'You are sure you are not too tired? If you wish to go back to the inn I will gladly come with you…'

Caroline gave her a searching look. 'I am very well, I thank you, Lavender, but I appreciate your concern. Do I gather from your reluctance that Frances has suggested we visit Hammonds? If *you* do not wish to go there and buy some more gloves, I shall come with *you* back to the inn…'

Lavender blushed. She was not at all sure how her sister-in-law had guessed that she had an aversion to Hammonds at present, nor was she going to ask.

'Oh no, I am very happy to go there,' she said

airily. 'I was only concerned that you should not tire yourself—'

'Very thoughtful, my love,' Caroline said with a smile, 'and I am sure that Mr Hammond will not be in Northampton today—'

Lavender shot out of the shop before Caroline could humiliate her further and before Frances should start asking awkward questions. The chill air on the street served to cool her red face a little. She reflected ruefully that Caroline was obviously some kind of clairvoyant, for she could swear that she had not mentioned Hammonds and in particular Mr Barney Hammond for at least ten days. Even when she had returned ignominiously from her accident in the wood, she had managed to skate adroitly over the fact that it was Barney who had found her there and escorted her home. She stared fiercely at a gold shawl in the shop window and told herself that she was being foolish. There should be no particular reason for her to avoid Barney Hammond, nor to seek him out, for that matter. She should just behave naturally.

Even so, when they reached the doorway of Hammond's Emporium, she was most reluctant to go in. It did not improve the situation that the first person they saw was Arthur Hammond himself, who looked first surprised and then unctuously satisfied to see them. He rushed forward, almost knocking over an elderly lady in his hurry to greet them.

'Ladies! How charming to see you! How may I be of assistance?'

It seemed that in very short order, every sales assistant in the shop was scurrying round to measure and cut—lace for Caroline, sarcenet for Lady Anne, stockings for Frances, which Hammond passed to her with a roguish smile. All the other customers, with their flannel petticoats and ribbons, were obliged to wait, whilst Hammond rubbed his hands and said how honoured he was to have such noble visitors, until Lavender left the shop in very disgust.

She stood on the pavement and gazed at the apothecary's shop next door whilst a feeling of relief crept through her that Barney had not been present. Then a voice said, 'How do you do, Miss Brabant? It is an unexpected pleasure to see you here in Northampton.'

Barnabas Hammond was standing before her in a coat of blue superfine, buff pantaloons and a pair of boots that Lavender suspected owed more to Hobys of London than the admittedly excellent shoemakers of Northampton. The coat fitted his broad shoulders without one superfluous wrinkle, and suited his tall figure to perfection. Lavender found herself staring and tried to stop, but seemed unable to do so. His dark hair was worn a little long and curled thickly over the collar of his jacket. He looked freshly shaved and smelled very faintly and deliciously of eau-de-cologne. Yet none of that was what really compelled her attention. Lavender puzzled, and came to the conclusion that it was somehow Barney's containment that was so attractive, the impression of raw power captured and held under control, but barely. He was not cut out to play the society fop, polished and perfumed. He was too physical a man for that. His appearance conjured up a dangerous vision, the image of him in the pool, the brown, muscular body, the water sliding over him… Or during the fencing match, his shirt sticking to his body as he moved with skill and grace…

Lavender swallowed hard and tried to summon up a polite social smile. The streets of Northampton were in no way an appropriate place for such wayward thoughts.

'Mr Hammond! How do you do, sir?'

'I am well, thank you.' There was the implication of a smile in Barney's voice. He did not say anything else, but watched her with those very dark eyes that always made Lavender feel strangely self-conscious. She could feel it now, feel her already shaky social skills slipping away from her. All she could think of was that she had made a complete fool of herself the last time they had met, and now she was set fair to do the same again. Her gaze fixed desperately on the parcel in his arms.

'You have been shopping, I see,' she said, with what she knew to be ghastly archness. 'Have you bought anything interesting?'

'I have been to the apothecary's shop for some remedies for my mother,' Barney said with a smile. 'I was in there when I saw you. She always gives me a commission, for she swears by Dr Anderson's Scotts Pills and Vegetable Syrup of de Velnos!'

'What maladies do they cure?' Lavender asked, fascinated by the slow amusement in his voice and the warmth in those dark eyes. Barney smiled and her heart gave a little skip.

'Just about everything, I believe!' he said cheerfully. 'Certainly my mama suffers from just about every disease known to man! She has a copy of *Solomon's Guide to Health* at home, Miss Brabant, and looks up every ailment in it! It gives her great pleasure to decide what she will suffer from next!'

Lavender giggled and tried to turn it into a cough. 'Oh dear. You do not sound very sympathetic, sir…'

'No.' The amusement died from Barney's face. 'Your pardon. I should not make a joke of it. Truth to tell, the apothecary's business has always fascinated me. Whilst there are any number of false remedies for sale, and some positively dangerous, I believe, there are some chemists and pharmacists who do the most interesting work. I should like—' He broke off, turning slightly away. 'I beg your pardon, Miss Brabant. I can become most tedious on the subject!'

Lavender opened her mouth to contradict him, but in that moment they were joined by the gentleman

whom Lavender had last seen pitting his fencing skill
so unsuccessfully against Barney that day in the forest. He was tall and fair, and at close quarters
Lavender could see that he had a twinkle in his blue
eyes and a humorous set to his mouth. Barney performed the introductions very smoothly.

'Miss Brabant, this is Mr James Oliver, a friend
of mine. Jamie, this is Miss Lavender Brabant.'

Mr Oliver bowed. 'Delighted to meet you, Miss
Brabant. I believe you must be another of the inhab-
itants of the Abbey villages? I rather think I recog-
nise the name—'

Lavender was just explaining where Hewly fitted
in when the rest of her party spilled out of the doorway, chattering excitedly about their purchases. They
broke off when they saw that Lavender had company.

'Mr Hammond! What a pleasant surprise!'
Caroline smiled at Barney and held out her hand.
'What brings you to Northampton, sir?'

'I am here on business,' Barney said, achieving an
elegant bow over her hand. 'How do you do, ma'am?
Ladies…'

Introductions were effected. James Oliver mentioned that they were going to the booksellers to collect tickets for a concert that night and they all fell
into step as Lady Anne invited the gentlemen to escort them back to the Bear inn on their way.

Whilst James chatted to Frances, Lady Anne and

Caroline engaged Barney in conversation. Lavender felt secretly chagrined. In a contrary fashion, she had been hoping he would walk beside her.

'Do you find much to amuse you in Northampton, Mr Hammond?' Lady Anne enquired. 'It is only a small town but it seems quite lively!'

Barney gave her his slow smile and Lavender was almost sure she saw Lady Anne blink under its impact. It seemed that no one was immune.

'There is certainly plenty to see and do, ma'am!' Barney was saying. 'Tonight we are promised for a concert at the guildhall, as James mentioned. It was a choice between the recital and a performer of magical illusions, but I prefer the music because I am forever trying to work out how the magic tricks are done! It ruins one's enjoyment!'

'You must be a scientific gentleman, Mr Hammond,' Lady Anne said, with a smile. 'For my part I am always fascinated by such sleight of hand and never pause to question how it comes about!'

They reached the Bear and found the gentlemen already waiting for them in the parlour. Whilst they all shook hands, Lady Anne seemed struck with a good idea.

'Mr Hammond, Mr Oliver, are you already engaged for Friday night? If not you must come to our ball! No, positively you must! It would be delightful!'

Lavender felt rather than saw Barney glance across

quickly at her. It seemed obvious to her that he was torn between a polite lie and a reluctant acceptance. Her heart sank as she decided his natural inclination would be to avoid the ball on her account.

'Well, ma'am, you are most kind…' Barney began, 'but I do not think—'

'Oh, come now, old fellow,' James interposed, with a lazy smile at Frances, 'don't disappoint the ladies!'

'Oh, please say you will come!' Frances had turned quite pink as she added her heartfelt pleas and received a quelling look from her mother for her pains. Lavender did not dare look at Barney again. Part of her wanted him to accept and the other half was ready to sink with embarrassment.

'For my part, I should be delighted, ma'am,' Mr Oliver said quickly, 'and I am sure that Barney will be able to drag himself away from business if he tries hard enough!'

'That's settled then,' Anne Covingham said briskly, but with a warm smile. 'We shall look forward to seeing you at Riding Park on Friday night. I will send someone over with cards for you.'

Farewells were said and the gentlemen went off in the direction of Lacey's booksellers. Frances positively bounced over to Lavender's side. 'Oh Lavender, you lucky creature to know Mr Hammond already! Is he not the most charming man! And so prodigiously attractive…'

Lavender raised her eyebrows. She had thought that it was James Oliver who had been commanding most of Frances's attention and found that she felt more than a little jealous of her new friend's interest in Barney Hammond. For surely Barney *was* prodigiously attractive but she did not wish everyone to think so. Frances was rattling on.

'And Mr Oliver! I declare we are so fortunate to meet not one but two delightful gentlemen!'

'Here, on the other hand, is an encounter less enjoyable,' Caroline said dryly. She put a hand on Lavender's arm. 'Don't look now, my love, but I see your cousin Julia is in town!'

Lavender turned to peer out of the window. A smart travelling coach had pulled up in the yard and was disgorging its occupants. The gentleman was quite elderly, greying and distinguished, but hanging on his arm was a younger woman whom Lavender recognised with a sinking heart.

'Oh no, Caro, I fear you are right! It *is* cousin Julia!'

The vision was dressed in vivid blue, in a robe trailing acres of lace and surely more suitable for the boudoir than the town. A matching blue hat framed a face of pink and white perfection with huge blue eyes. Ringlets of guinea gold blew in the breeze.

The perfection was marred somewhat by a heavy frown, and even from inside the parlour, Lavender could hear her cousin's hectoring voice as she harangued a servant.

'What do you mean, the private parlour is occupied? Tell them to go elsewhere! We are far more important—'

'Who is *that?*' Frances Covingham whispered in Lavender's ear, staring hard. 'Why, she looks like a demi-rep!'

Anne Covingham, catching the edge of this whisper, shot her daughter a furious look. 'Frances, come away from the window—'

'I fear it is too late for escape,' Caroline said sepulchrally. 'They are coming this way—'

There was a step in the passage and the door swung open. Julia's china blue eyes swept over them all and she let out a little shriek.

'Lud! Caroline? Lavender! Lewis…'

Caroline had already stepped forward, with a mixture of resignation and courtesy, to greet the new arrivals.

'Julia! How do you do? This is a…surprise…'

'She is a distant cousin of ours,' Lavender whispered to Frances. 'Mrs Chessford—'

'Oh, I have heard of her!' Frances's eyes were bright with amusement. 'Mama calls her a bird of paradise masquerading as—'

'Delighted to meet you, Mrs Chessford,' Anne Covingham said hastily, stepping forward, hand outstretched. 'We have all heard such a great deal about you! I believe that you were hoping for a private parlour? By great good chance we were just leaving…'

The others all gathered their purchases together hurriedly. Lavender thought that Julia looked quite torn, on the one hand thanking Lady Anne graciously for her kindness and on the other evidently annoyed to be denied such august company.

'I shall call on you at Riding Park to express my obligation,' she gushed, grasping Lord Freddie warmly by the hand. 'It is so delightful to have some acquaintance in the locality!'

Lavender thought she saw Anne Covingham blench. She shepherded them all out to the carriages in short order and soon they were rattling back to Riding Park.

'The worst of it,' Caroline said gloomily, speaking for them all, 'is that Julia *will* call at the Park and will be impossibly difficult to shake off! I should not say it, but she is like a nasty rash—all over one and inducing unpleasant humours!' And they all collapsed into laughter.

Chapter Four

'This is all very dull,' Julia Chessford whispered in Lavender's ear. 'I had expected far better! This is just country neighbours of the Covinghams and not a coronet amongst them!'

They were sitting in the ballroom at Riding Park, watching a few couples circle the floor in a stately minuet. Up on the wooden minstrels' gallery a string quartet was playing and around the room the buzz of conversation was rising as the guests arrived and the servants circulated with a very fine champagne.

Lavender gave her cousin a look of comprehensive dislike. She had just been thinking the occasion very pleasant, and felt that Julia was more than fortunate to have been invited in the first place.

After the encounter at the inn, Julia had positively forced herself on their notice. She had taken advantage by calling every day, had proclaimed a fulsome fondness for Caroline and Lavender which the latter found quite nauseous, and had contrived to invite herself to the ball without so much as an 'if you please.'

Julia had grown up at Hewly as Admiral Brabant's ward and Lavender had known from the start that she was a sly, devious girl who would wheedle her way into company simply for what she could gain. Julia had been secretly betrothed to Lewis when they had both been in their green days, but she had thrown Lewis over for his elder brother Andrew, only to elope with Andrew's best friend instead. They had not heard from her again until her husband was dead and his fortune frittered away, then Julia had come to Hewly to try to extract money from her guardian and had used the excuse of the Admiral's last illness to foist herself on them once again. For a time Lavender had feared that Lewis would succumb to Julia's charm again, and had been relieved as well as delighted when Lewis's choice had rested on Caroline instead. Julia had left Hewly under a cloud when her attempts to blackmail the Admiral had been exposed, and for the best part of a year they had not heard from her. And now here she was again, like a bad penny…

'I am amazed at Lady Anne permitting her daughter to associate with tradesmen,' Julia continued, a sneer in her voice as she nodded across the ballroom at Frances Covingham, who was dancing the cotillion with Barney Hammond. Lavender felt the twin irritations of a stab of jealousy and a rush of dislike for Julia, and shifted uncomfortably on her rout chair. Barney had not asked her to dance yet—if he was going to ask at all—and it did not help that he appeared very popular with Lady Anne's female guests. Lavender thought that Barney looked very striking in his evening clothes. More than that, he moved with an unconscious confidence and easy grace that made him look quite at home.

'I suppose he dresses like a gentleman,' Julia said, echoing Lavender's thoughts, 'but that is only to be expected when one's father is a draper! Extraordinary! Northampton merchants in the Covinghams' ballroom! It takes more than a fortune to wash away the smell of the shop!'

'Well, of course, you would know that, Julia!' Lavender said, pricked into retaliation by Julia's niggling. She knew it was childish, but since Julia's own father had been in trade she thought her snobbery the outside of enough.

Julia, however, had a hide as thick as an elephant. 'Well, I suppose the Covingham chit may be hanging out for a fortune and Hammond could probably buy up everyone in the room! But what is that to the purpose when he has no breeding? The Covinghams may not be high in the instep but surely they would never permit their daughter to marry into trade!'

'I think you are jumping to extraordinary conclusions, Julia,' Lavender said coldly. 'Miss Covingham has danced but once with Mr Hammond and looks in no danger of eloping! Besides, she has danced twice with Mr Oliver and even you must admit he is a very eligible *parti!*'

'Yes.' Julia's blue eyes narrowed thoughtfully. 'I confess I could develop a *tendre* there myself, for Mr Oliver is very good-looking and has all the connections that Mr Hammond lacks! He is a sad flirt, however, and faithless as the day is long!'

Lavender's lips twitched. Once again she felt the pot was calling the kettle black, for Julia's lack of fidelity was breathtaking.

Julia was still watching Frances and Barney Hammond as they danced the cotillion.

'Of course, the inclination to bolt does run in the Covingham family! Harriet Covingham threatened to run off with John Farley and now the *on dit* is that she is about to run away with her latest lover—'

Lavender sighed and fidgeted, wishing that either some gentleman would take pity on her and ask her to dance, or Caroline would return from her coze with Anne Covingham and rescue her. It was particularly galling that she had had no offers to dance, for she had thought she was quite in looks this evening. Frances had helped her choose her most flattering gown, a lavender silk of simple but stylish design, and she had arranged her hair in an elegant Grecian knot. She had felt reasonably happy with her appearance until Julia had arrived, tiny and stunningly beautiful in soft rose pink, her hair a mass of golden curls. Julia had allowed her blue gaze to linger on Lavender with a certain degree of pity and her cousin had felt her warm glow of confidence shrivel a little. And now the gentlemen did not ask her to dance…

'Would you care to dance, Lavender?'

Julia smirked as Lewis Brabant bowed in front of his sister. 'Lud, dancing with your own brother now, Lavender! How slow!'

Lewis gave his cousin a look of disdain. 'Your servant, Julia. I see that Lord Leverstoke has taken refuge in the card room! I am surprised you could not persuade him to dance with you!'

Julia flushed a little. She was evidently sensitive about her elderly beau, whom Lavender had heard was still married to someone else. Lewis gave Lavender his arm and turned smartly away.

'We do not have to dance,' he said with a smile, as they drew away from Julia, 'but Caro suggested I bring you over to her anyway. It is a pity that Lady Anne's manners are so good that she felt obliged to invite Julia tonight! Our cousin is clearly as much of an encroaching mushroom as ever!'

Lavender giggled. 'You are ungallant, Lewis!' she chided. 'Lord Leverstoke seems to dote on her!'

Lewis shrugged his broad shoulders. 'Leverstoke always had poor judgement! And he has no money either, so I do not anticipate Julia wasting her time

on him for long! Someone younger and richer would
be more to her taste!'

Lavender's glance slid away to Barney Hammond,
who had finished his dance with Frances and was
being introduced to another blushing débutante by
Anne Covingham. The sight made Lavender feel
sadly out of sorts. Turning her shoulder, she took a
seat by Caroline, and Lewis strolled off to fetch them
some more champagne.

Her sister-in-law welcomed her warmly. 'We
thought we should rescue you, my love, for you
looked as glum as a wet Tuesday! Who does Julia
have her knife into this time?'

Lavender smiled and felt a little better. 'I fear she
was being cruel about poor Mr Hammond! Of all the
hypocrites, when her own father made his fortune
from trade!'

'I can see you feel very strongly about it!'
Caroline observed, raising her brows. Lavender realised that she had probably given away more than she
intended. She blushed and tried to moderate her tone.

'Well, it is all so unfair, Caro! Mr Hammond has
a pleasing address, and just because his father is a
draper…'

'Yes,' Caroline smoothed the skirts of her amber
gown, 'it is unfair. I should know, for I spent many
years being slighted as an upper servant!' She smiled
at Lavender. 'That is why the Covinghams are such
particular friends, for they never made me feel in any

way inferior. But it is a sad fact that most of society is not so generous! I deplore the gradations of snobbery but I see them all around me!'

Lavender slumped a little. She did not know why she felt the difficulty of Barney Hammond's position so keenly, but Julia's words had made her burn with fury. And it was not even as though Barney had pushed himself on their notice as Julia herself had done. Lavender told herself that she hated Julia's conceit, but at the back of her mind was a little voice that asked her if she was any better. She remembered her encounter with Barney that first night in the wood, and how she had thought his conversation impertinent. Had that not been because she was so sure of their relative positions as draper's son and admiral's daughter? And yet there was nothing so clear-cut about her feelings for him now...

Lavender squeezed her fan so tightly that two of the struts splintered. She pushed it into her bag, feeling even more annoyed.

'Of course,' Caroline continued, as Lewis came back to them with the refreshments, 'there is another reason that Julia dislikes Mr Hammond!'

Lewis handed her a glass of champagne and looked enquiring. 'Pray divulge it, my dear,' he said with a grin, sitting down beside them, 'for both Lavender and I are now on the edge of our chairs!'

'Well...' Caroline said. She sat forward a little, her eyes sparkling. 'I do believe that our cousin took Mr

Hammond in dislike after he…' she paused, 'after he rejected her advances!'

Lewis raised his eyebrows quizzically. Lavender drew a sharp breath.

'Oh Caro, no! Say she did not make a set at him!'

Caroline shrugged. 'Why not? She would scarce be the first lady to try!'

'Do you have any evidence for this theory, my love,' Lewis said lazily, 'or is it just scurrilous gossip on your part?'

Caroline looked hurt. 'Now Lewis… You know I do not gossip!' She bent a little closer to them. 'No, we were in Hammond's shop one day, and Mr Barnabas Hammond was dealing with Julia's requests for ribbons and bows, when suddenly I heard her remark that he was a fine figure of a man and a good advertisement for his father's tailoring!' Caroline's eyes twinkled. 'Well, I knew I was not supposed to be party to the conversation, but at that I leant closer!'

'I am sure you did…' Lewis murmured dryly.

Lavender patted her sister-in-law's hand. 'Take no notice of him! I want to hear what happened—'

'I am sure you do!' Lewis said ironically. Both girls glared at him.

'If you wish to spoil the story, pray stand further off, my dear!' Caroline said severely to her husband. She turned back to Lavender. 'Well, then Julia said that she had a particular commission for him, and would he care to come out to Hewly to consult with her privately! I do not think that *that* could be misconstrued!'

Lavender stared at her, her eyes huge. 'Caro! And Mr Hammond—'

Caroline started to laugh. 'I will never forget this bit! Barnabas Hammond said that he was grateful for her attention, but he was sorry, his father always dealt with the older ladies! I do not believe Julia ever forgave him! After that she always made me run the errands to the drapers!'

Lavender gave a snort of laughter. Even Lewis was hastily trying to repress a guffaw. There was something exquisitely pleasurable about Julia, who had made all their lives miserable with her high-handed ways and niggling remarks, receiving the set down that she so richly deserved.

'Oh dear, how dreadful!' she said, wiping the tears of laughter from her eyes. 'And truly, we should not laugh, but…' Her shoulders shook as she tried to get her mirth under control.

'Well,' Lewis said, 'I shall look on Hammond with even more kindness in future! I always thought him a man of great good sense, and here we have the proof!'

A half hour later, Lavender had just resigned herself to the fact that she would be sitting amongst the chaperones all evening, when James Oliver approached to ask her to partner him in the set of country dances that was just forming. After that, Lavender was besieged with partners, as though the company had only been waiting for one gentleman to approach her before they all rushed in. She was a good dancer and acquitted herself well, and found the social dialogue required on such occasions quite undemanding. One could not really strike up a proper conversation, for the steps of the dance were forever separating the partners, but Lavender reflected that this was perhaps all to the good. She had heard quite enough about Mr Henshaw's pack of gun dogs and she was not terribly interested in Mr Salton's new curricle. She remembered that her chaperone during the London Season had told her that a lady should always appear to find a gentleman's conversation fascinating, but Lavender thought this so much nonsense. She had quickly seen that a gentleman was treated as though he was even more charming if he had the good fortune to be an Earl or a Duke.

Mr Salton was still holding forth about the brilliance of his team when Lavender saw Barney Hammond approaching them across the ballroom. It had not escaped her notice that he had danced twice already with Miss Covingham and that the irrepressible Frances had been very reluctant to lose his company.

Barney bowed very formally to her, but there was a smile in his eyes.

'Miss Brabant, I have been hoping against hope that you would still be free to grant me the supper dance? I would be honoured.'

Lavender was about to agree, when Mr Salton cleared his throat meaningfully. 'Don't think that would be quite the thing, old chap. After all, there is an order of precedence at these events, don't you know, and for you to lead in Miss Brabant...' He let the sentence hang with just the faintest implication of a sneer.

Lavender saw Barney flush as the insult struck home, saw the flash of pure fury in his eyes before he fought down his anger and gave the younger man a bland smile.

'Thank you for your advice, old fellow.' There was more than a little sarcasm in his own voice now. 'I was, however, addressing Miss Brabant...'

He turned back to Lavender and for a second she saw the hint of uncertainty in his face, before he squared his shoulders as though preparing to receive a set down. That brief moment when she saw his vulnerability gave her the strangest feeling inside.

'Thank you, Mr Hammond,' she said a little tremulously. 'I should be delighted to dance with you.'

The music had already struck up. Barney offered her his arm and led her into the nearest set.

'Thank you for your kindness, Miss Brabant,' he murmured, as they took their place in the dance. 'It was most generous in you—'

Lavender had recovered herself and could not bear to hear him sound so humble. 'I am neither generous nor kind, Mr Hammond,' she said crisply, 'except in general terms, of course. I *wished* to dance with you!'

For a moment Barney looked startled by such a frank admission, then he rallied.

'Well, in that case—'

'And pray do not thank me again,' Lavender finished, thinking that she may as well be hanged for a sheep as a lamb, 'for I did nothing but consult my own inclination! There! We may be comfortable again!'

Barney's face was grave, shadowed. It seemed that he could not shake off Mr Salton's insults so lightly. 'Do you not judge as the rest of the world then, Miss Brabant, on rank and consequence and such matters?'

'So much nonsense!' Lavender said, knowing she sounded just like her late papa, the Admiral. 'A fine thing it would be for me to apply society's rules when I am one of those it most disapproves of, for valuing books above looks!'

Barney's expression lightened as he laughed. 'And where do accomplishment and intellect rate in the eyes of the world, Miss Brabant?'

'Why, almost nowhere, I believe! Accomplishment in a female is quite a good thing as long as it is restricted to drawing prettily and playing well, but it cannot compensate for good looks!'

'You are an outspoken critic,' Barney said slowly.

'Of society's rules? Well, they are so foolish and fickle they deserve my derision!' Lavender smiled at him. There was still a small frown between his eyes but it melted as his gaze met hers and something warmer took its place. Lavender suddenly felt unaccountably hot. She fell silent, pretending that she was concentrating on the steps of the dance.

Dancing with Barney was more disturbing than she had anticipated; the touch of his hand stirred memories of their encounter in the wood, and once again, his proximity had a wholly disconcerting effect on her. Lavender was used to being in control of her emotions and she found this weakness deeply unsettling.

'Perhaps we should conform to convention and speak of more commonplace matters, Mr Hammond?' she said, a little at random. 'Are you enjoying the ball?'

'Yes, indeed. The Covinghams are very pleasant people,' Barney said promptly. 'Your friend, Miss Covingham, is a delightful girl, is she not?'

Lavender felt the same sinking feeling that she remembered from the parties and balls of her London Season. Just as soon as she had thought she had found a pleasant gentleman with whom to converse in a sensible fashion, it seemed that he only wished to discuss her prettier companions. That it was Barney Hammond talking to her this time only seemed to make matters worse.

'Oh, Frances is the kindest creature imaginable,' she said, trying to keep her tone light, 'and a true friend to me since we first arrived here!'

'She tells me that she is much in awe of you,' Barney said, with a smile. 'She said that she wishes she were even half as accomplished, though given your recent remarks, you may not rate that a compliment!'

Lavender smiled. 'Well, I know Frances would never deal in Spanish coin, so I am grateful that she at least values my attainments! But then with Caro as her governess, it is no surprise that she sees the value of useful accomplishments!'

The final flourish of the music swept them into their respective bow and curtsey, and it was then time to go into supper. Caroline waved at them across the room.

'Do you wish to take supper with us?' she asked, slipping her hand through Lavender's arm. 'The most diverting thing—I have just been talking to the odious Mr Salton! He was chatting pleasantly until I said that I had worked for the Covingham family, upon which he started, bowed slightly and said that he had mistaken me for a friend of the family! He then walked off—'

'And I almost ran him through!' Lewis finished, somewhat grimly. 'Insufferable young puppy!'

'Anne tells me that he has just inherited his uncle's estate and is all puffed up with his own consequence!' Caroline said. 'Never mind. Let us talk on more agreeable topics!'

They chatted pleasantly about Northampton, its entertainments and amusements, until supper was ended and Barney excused himself to dance with another of Anne Covingham's protégées.

'Mr Hammond is very popular tonight,' Caroline observed idly, 'and most confident in this setting. He is a most unusual young man. Do you not think so, Lavender?'

'Oh, he is very pleasant,' Lavender agreed brightly, hoping she did not sound as though she were trying too hard to sound careless.

'Damned with faint praise!' Caroline said, but there was a twinkle in her eye.

It was towards the end of the ball that Lavender had the misfortune of bumping into the graceless Mr Salton again. She had gone upstairs to fetch a wrap for Caroline and had paused in the Long Gallery to admire some of the Covingham portraits on the way back. There was a very fine likeness of Lady Anne as a young girl, a flattering portrait of Lord Freddie, and beside it a small picture of a gentleman in a gilt frame. Lavender had almost passed it by, for it was in a dark corner, but something caught her eye. She stepped a little closer.

The gentleman in the picture was young and dark, with an inscrutable expression that seemed strangely familiar. Lavender was just puzzling over where she had seen him before when she heard a footstep beside her and someone's arm insinuated itself about her waist. Lavender turned sharply to confront Mr Salton's flushed face and recoiled from the stench of wine on his breath.

'Miss Brabant! Loitering with intent, ma'am?'

Lavender tried to step back, but he held her firmly.

'I have no notion what you mean, sir!' she said, with distaste. 'Kindly leave me alone!'

Mr Salton leered meaningfully. 'No need to play coy, ma'am! I know that you were waiting for me!'

He leant forward clumsily and Lavender realised belatedly and with horror that he was about to try and kiss her. She turned her head sharply and felt him press his wet lips to her neck rather than her mouth. She shuddered.

'Mr Salton! You forget yourself! Unhand me at once!' She wanted to sound authoritative but was aware that instead she sounded breathless with outrage and surprise. She struggled, kicking his shins as hard as she could in her ball slippers, and slapping his grasping hands aside with her fan. The treatment was probably not painful but it was effective. Mr Salton's already flushed face turned a deeper red and he yelped with fury, grabbing Lavender's wrist.

'You little vixen! You'll pay for that—'

'Can I be of service, Miss Brabant? Mrs Brabant sent me to find you—she was somewhat concerned that you had been gone for some time...'

Lavender closed her eyes for an agonised moment. The measured tones could only be those of Barney Hammond, who seemed to be making a habit of rescuing her these days. Her face burned with a mixture of embarrassment and fury to have been found in such an undignified situation. Nor was Mr Salton helping the case, for he was evidently so inebriated that he could barely grasp what was happening and was still holding on to her wrist. She saw Barney's dark eyes narrow murderously as he took in Mr Salton's drunken state and the fact that he was still gripping her arm. As she tried to free herself, Barney said silkily, 'Unhand the lady, Salton. You are making a nuisance of yourself.'

Mr Salton's hand dropped away from Lavender as he turned unsteadily to face his new adversary. 'Don't presume to tell me what to do, Hammond,' he sneered. 'What can the jumped up son of a draper possibly know about polite society—'

Barney's face was expressionless. 'My antecedents have nothing to do with your bad manners, Salton. Stand aside.'

Mr Salton stepped back and took a wild swing at Barney. The blow failed to connect since he was so drunk he could barely see straight. Lavender drew a sharp breath. For a moment, Barney looked so dangerous that she was certain he was about to hit Salton and she was sure that his aim would be considerably more direct. Then Barney paused, put one hand on

Salton's shoulder and simply pushed the younger man. The drink did the rest. Salton staggered, cannoned off the edge of the window embrasure, and slumped quietly on the floor. Lavender pressed both hands to her mouth.

'Oh no! How dreadful!'

'But infinitely better than it might have been.' Barney's face was still expressionless.

He took a couple of steps towards her. 'I hope that you are not hurt, Miss Brabant?'

All Lavender's mortification came flooding back. 'Not in the least, sir. Thank you for your prompt intervention. I am sorry that it was necessary.'

'So am I,' Barney said a little grimly. 'If you will loiter in poorly lit corridors, Miss Brabant—'

Lavender, suffering from shock and embarrassment, reacted strongly to the injustice of this. It had not occurred to her that any of the blame might attach to her. 'I merely paused to take a look at the portraits, sir! I cannot see that that gives Mr Salton the right to think that he may force his attentions on me!'

'Not the right, but the opportunity,' Barney said, with an expressive lift of his dark brows. 'You seem to be forever wandering into trouble, do you not, Miss Brabant? Walking in the forest at night, getting caught in traps during the day, facilitating the attentions of a drunken womaniser—'

Lavender flushed with fury. She took an impulsive

step forward. 'How dare you, sir! Your observations on my conduct are discourteous—'

She found that her anger had propelled her far closer to him than she had intended, and that an acute physical awareness of him suddenly overcame her. The words dried in her throat and she stared up into the dark eyes that were suddenly so close to her own. She saw the moment when his own expression changed, focusing more intently on her, setting her heart racing. He took a step towards her, the final step. They were very close now. Lavender could not tear her gaze away from him.

Barney's hand was already on her arm when there was the sound of a step along the stone corridor and they broke apart, the moment shattered.

Caroline's voice said, 'There you are! I had quite given up on my wrap—' She broke off as her gaze fell on the recumbent form of Mr Salton. 'Oh dear, I see—your handiwork, Mr Hammond?'

Lavender heard Barney take a deep breath. 'I can claim little credit, I fear, ma'am,' he said. 'The gentleman was so inebriated he could barely stand.'

Caroline tutted. 'Well, let us leave him here until Lord Freddie's servants throw him out! Mr Hammond, would you be so good as to escort us back to the ballroom?'

'Gladly, ma'am.' Barney stepped back with scrupulous courtesy to allow Lavender to precede him.

She was very aware that he was avoiding looking directly at her. His expression was quite blank.

'I think I shall retire,' she said quickly. 'I have no taste for further dancing. Good night, Mr Hammond. Good night, Caro.'

She sped away before Caroline could demur, hurried along the corridor to her room, and threw herself on the bed, lying back and staring at the canopy. Her heart was still beating quickly, the residual excitement still fizzing in her blood.

Another second, and she knew Barney Hammond would have kissed her. She had wanted him to, ached for him to take her in his arms. She was still trembling at the thought, could still feel the touch of his hand and see the concentrated look in those dark eyes... Lavender rolled over, pressing her hot face into the pillow. The same heat had infused her blood when she had seen Barney at the pool in the forest. He was as prodigiously attractive as Frances Covingham had said, and she could not deny it.

She lay there breathing in the sweet scent of lavender from the sheets and listening to the faint sound of music from the ballroom below. What was happening to her? It was one thing to admire a personable man, or to be drawn to the conversation of a man of sense and integrity. It was quite another to feel such passion, both physical and intellectual. She had never experienced the like of it before and it was utterly perplexing. Lavender lay still, conjuring up the memory of Barney's touch, his voice. She shivered. She knew she was in danger of losing her heart and it was a frightening thought. For all her brave words against snobbery, she knew that such an unequal match could never be.

'Oh Lavender, I swear I have lost my heart and it can never be!' Frances Covingham was shredding a tiny white handkerchief between her fingers and was obliged to borrow Lavender's considerably larger one to wipe away her tears. 'Mama has warned me—gently, but warned me nonetheless—that he is too old and quite ineligible! I feel so desolate I think I shall cast myself into the lake!'

Frances accompanied the words with a look over her shoulder at the Riding Park lake, which glittered placidly in the midday sun. It was the afternoon following the ball and the two girls were sitting on a bench that was prettily positioned under some weeping willow. A family of ducks fluttered and splashed in the shallows. It was a tranquil scene, but Frances was far from calm. She had positively dragged Lavender away from the rest of the party in order to unburden her heart to her and Lavender felt ill equipped for the role of confidant.

Lavender had not slept particularly well, for her dreams had been snatched and full of images of Barney Hammond. Unlike Frances, who managed to look desolate but pretty, Lavender knew that she simply looked wan. And now, to hear Frances speaking of her tender feelings for Barney almost broke her heart.

'I have never met such an interesting and personable man,' Frances lamented, another tear rolling down her cheek. 'Last night—it must have been after you had retired, dearest Lavender—we sat and talked for hours! I felt so warm and so comfortable and so *happy*—'

She gave a miserable sniff.

'Perhaps your mama might relent,' Lavender said, feeling like a traitor, though whether to herself or to her friend she was not quite sure. 'Although, Frances, I must allow that Lady Anne is in the right of it. Your grandfather was a Duke and you are very eligible, whereas he—'

'I do not see that he is at all ineligible!' Frances disputed hotly. 'He has air and address and besides, his family is as good as mine!'

Lavender frowned, wondering if she had missed something. Frances seemed so distressed that she did not wish to add to her misery, but she could not agree.

'And now this morning Mama tells me that I must not see him again,' Frances finished, 'for she says that I am too young to form a lasting attachment and he has a reputation as a flirt—'

Lavender looked at her in astonishment. Whatever the charges that could be levelled at Barney

Hammond, this was not one of them. 'A flirt! Surely not! I have never observed Mr Hammond behave in such a way!'

Frances's green eyes opened very wide. 'Mr Hammond! Well, of course Mr Hammond is not a flirt! But I have heard that Mr Oliver has a reputation for it, although with me,' she blushed, 'he was the perfect soul of propriety even when I wished him not to be!'

Lavender frowned again. Her head was beginning to ache a little. The sun seemed very bright.

'I beg your pardon, Frances, but is it Mr Oliver for whom you have formed this attachment rather than Mr Hammond? I thought—' She broke off, deciding that there was no point in confusing the issue further. Frances was already looking at her with eyes wide with incredulity.

'Of course it is Mr Oliver! Who else? Really, Lavender, have you not been listening to a word I was saying?'

'No doubt it was very vexatious of me,' Lavender agreed meekly, 'but I was confused. After all, you had danced several times with Mr Hammond—'

'Yes, and Mr Potts and that odious Mr Salton! What is that to the purpose, pray? I sat and talked to Mr Oliver—James…' She blushed again, 'for hours, and he was so charming and kind to me! But Mama says that he is a hardened flirt and that she will not have another of her daughters making a foolish match and so…' she gave a little sob '…I am not to see him again!'

She held the soaking handkerchief forlornly in her hand, and Lavender rummaged in her reticule and produced a second one. 'There! How fortunate that I should have two! But pray do not cry any more, Frances, for it makes your nose quite pink! What if Mr Oliver were to call to pay his compliments and you are sitting out here with eyes and nose as red as a white rabbit?'

Lavender felt quite heartless as she spoke, but this was undoubtedly the best way to calm Frances, who was much struck by the idea of looking ugly. She wiped her eyes for a final time and took a deep breath.

'I suppose you are right. A melancholy air—without the tears—might be the very thing!'

'Precisely!' Lavender spoke bracingly. 'I am truly sorry that you needs must suffer for your sister's indiscretions, Frances, but perhaps Lady Anne will relent if she sees you behave in a sensible way! And if Mr Oliver is also steadfast in his affections—well, who knows…?'

Frances grasped her hand. 'Lavender, will you carry a letter to Mr Oliver for me? You could give it to Mr Hammond, for they are friends, after all, and Mr Hammond could pass a note on…'

Lavender's heart sank. Evidently Frances's idea of sensible behaviour and her own were poles apart.

'I do not think that a very good idea, Frances! Only think what would happen if your mama discovered you in a clandestine correspondence—'

'Oh please!' Frances's big green eyes pleaded with her. 'A letter can do no harm! Why, Mama should commend my industry, for she knows I hate writing letters!'

Lavender wriggled uncomfortably. She hated having to play a discouraging role, but she knew it was a bad idea to encourage Frances's hopes.

'I do not think that your mama would see it that way, Frances! And truly, it is not a very good idea!'

Lavender broke off. It was difficult to counsel sense to Frances when the idea actually held some appeal. To be the courier for Frances's letters to James Oliver, and have an excuse to see Barney Hammond again without having to buy another unnecessary pair of gloves... Lavender shook her head sharply. She knew that now she was just being foolish. If James Oliver was not an acceptable suitor for the granddaughter of a Duke, Barney Hammond was even less so for an Admiral's daughter. Besides, Frances did at least have some grounds for believing her feelings reciprocated. Lavender gazed at the sparkling lake and reflected miserably that she had no such basis for believing that Barney liked her. He had been courteous, kind even, and she had imagined that he might have wanted to kiss her, but that was all it was—imagination. And it was high time she accepted the truth.

Chapter Five

They left Riding Park two days later, sped on their way by good wishes and promises to visit from all the Covingham family. Frances had hugged Lavender and sworn that she would write, despite reminding her that she was the very worst correspondent in the whole world. The Covinghams planned to stay another two to three weeks in the country before making their way to London for the Little Season, and Frances was torn between high delight at the thought of her début in society and continued melancholy over her feelings for Mr Oliver.

The carriage was comfortable and Caroline dozed a little as they made slow progress along the narrow lanes. Lavender stared out of the window, and Lewis read one of the books that he had stopped to collect in Northampton. He had also picked up a parcel for Barney Hammond whilst he was there, for the bookseller, knowing that the Brabants were from Steep Abbot, had asked if they would undertake the delivery. Lavender wished that Lewis had refused but her brother, ever obliging, had cheerfully taken the commission.

Lavender looked at the parcel for Barney and, despite herself, wondered what it contained. Perhaps it was another medical dictionary for his mother, or some work of fiction for his sister. She remembered his references to his studies and wondered suddenly if these were academic books, and whether this was another of Barney's secrets. Perhaps he read Byron of an evening, seated in the drawing-room of the fine house that the Hammonds owned in Abbot Quincey. She tried to imagine it—for a moment she actually tried to place herself there, before the fire, with her botanical sketches and her works of scientific reference. Then her imagination fixed upon her sharing a fireside with Arthur Hammond, and her mind shuddered at the picture. Decidedly that would not do. Whichever fortunate young lady ended up as Barney's choice, she would have to love him a great deal to tolerate such a father-in-law.

Lavender looked out across the fields. The hedges and trees were fading from red and gold to the bare brown of winter. She usually loved the turning of the year, but just at the moment it made her feel sad. She looked up to see that Lewis had put down his book and was regarding her solemnly.

'What is it, sis? You look blue-devilled!'

Lavender smiled at the childhood appellation. 'I suppose it is just the loss of company. I had not expected to get pleasure from our visit to Riding Park, yet I had a prodigiously enjoyable time of it!'

Lewis nodded. 'Yes, it was most agreeable. And now we are thrown back on our own company—'

'Well, it will suffice!' Lavender suddenly felt more cheerful. 'I shall enjoy seeing Hewly again and besides, if we are short of company we may always invite Julia to stay—'

They laughed together.

'You may mock,' Caroline said sleepily, uncurling from her corner, 'but I heard her say that she would call! And she is still a sort of cousin, for all her misdemeanours!'

They started to discuss the ball.

'It is strange, is it not,' Caroline said, as the carriage rattled along, picking up speed now, 'how a man so pushing as Arthur Hammond should have produced a son as charming as Barney. One would think that he would not have it in him!'

Her words stirred a memory in Lavender's mind, a picture of herself taking tea with Nanny Pryor in the cottage on the estate where her old nurse had moved in her retirement. It had been two years ago, or perhaps three. They had been chatting and Lavender had idly said to the nurse that the Hammonds all had very distinctive dark good looks,

apart from Arthur Hammond, who was fair and
florid. And Nanny Pryor had poured the tea into the
flowered china cups and had said that the Hammonds
had all been fair in the male line until Arthur
Hammond's grandfather had married a Spanish girl,
and that Barney Hammond had inherited his looks
from his mother. Lavender could remember the
pursed look on Nanny Pryor's face, the prim expression that always preceded a major piece of gossip.
Then, sure enough, the nurse had said that Barney
was really Hammond's nephew and not his son at
all...

'I had heard that Barney is not Hammond's real
son—' Lavender said thoughtfully, breaking off at
the look of astonishment on the faces of Lewis and
Caroline. 'At least, that is the rumour,' she added, a
little hesitantly, 'but I have no notion if it is true...'

Lewis was frowning. 'I have never heard that tale,
Lavender. Where did you get it from?'

'Nanny Pryor told me,' Lavender said, blushing to
be repeating gossip. 'She said that Eliza Hammond
was Barney's mother, making Arthur Hammond his
uncle, not his father. No one knew who his real father
was, but there are those who say that it was the
Marquis of Sywell...'

Lewis whistled. 'Well, there are enough of
Sywell's brats about the county, it's true! What became of Eliza Hammond herself?'

'She died in childbirth and never spoke the name

of her lover,' Lavender said. 'At least that is what Nanny Pryor said. Apparently the Hammonds took the child as their own and never spoke of it again. I had almost forgot the tale until just now.'

Caroline raised her eyebrows. 'It's an intriguing story! It would certainly explain why Hammond treats Barney as a type of glorified shop manager rather than a true son!'

The others looked at her enquiringly. 'Well,' Caroline pointed out, 'have you never observed that Hammond has sent his second son—his eldest son, if the tale is true—away to university whilst poor Barney is expected to work in the shop? Hammond has been so successful and is such a social climber, that he grooms his children as ladies and gentlemen! The boys have a tutor and the girls a governess, and he clearly feels the shop not good enough for them. What man would not, having achieved what he has done? And this gives him the best of both worlds, for whilst they may inherit his fortune, Barney will be there to carry on the business!'

Lavender turned to look out of the window. She did not wish her face to betray her. She had given little thought to the old tale before, for the Abbey villages were always full of gossip, but now it made her wonder—and it made her burn with indignation for Barney. She could not see why he should be made to suffer twice over, once for being illegitimate, and a second time because he was obliged to do Hammond's bidding to earn his keep. That would explain why he kept so much a secret from his family, the adoptive relatives with whom he did not quite fit.

'I cannot see that it would be much advantage to be another of Sywell's by-blows,' Lewis was saying. 'Unlikely that a man would inherit any good looks or charm from that quarter!'

'Do you think that they will ever discover who murdered the Marquis?' Caroline asked idly, with a little shiver. 'Ugh! It gives me the horrors to think of someone creeping about that old barn of an Abbey intent on murder!'

Lavender turned away again. This was one conversation that she certainly did not intend to join, for it pricked her conscience. There were certain things that she knew, things she had seen, that the Lord Lieutenant who was investigating the Marquis's murder would be very interested to know. But she could never tell...

'I do declare we are become as good gossips as anyone in the kingdom,' Caroline said, on a yawn. 'It must be the Covinghams' influence! Lord, I am tired, though! I am glad we are nearly home!'

The coach had almost reached Steep Abbott now. Lavender sat back and watched the trees of Steep Wood press in on the road. In the distance she could see the curve of the river. It was familiar and beautiful, and it did a little to assuage the ache in her heart. There was no doubt, though, that the remedy for her indisposition lay in her own hands. She would have to avoid Barney Hammond, at least until this foolish *tendre* she had developed had faded away. Then she might be able to treat him with equanimity. Now she had no such chance.

The following day saw Lavender walking into Abbot Quincey, in direct contradiction of what she knew to be her own best interests. Lewis had originally intended to take the gig out and drive round the estate, visiting Abbot Quincey afterwards to deliver Barney's books and make a number of other calls. However, the tenant of Hewlton, a farm some three miles away, had called on Lewis urgently to discuss the problem of a fallen tree that had breached the estate wall. The two men were closeted in Lewis's study and Caroline had suggested gently that Lavender might like to visit the Percevals—and hand over the books on the way.

Lavender had wanted to refuse but could not think of an adequate excuse. Part of her wanted to confide her feelings in Caroline anyway, but the other part was in such a turmoil that she knew not what she might say. In the end she had agreed, and had taken the package of books and an offering of apples from the Newton Wonder tree for Lady Perceval.

Barney was serving in the shop when she went in, and was just handing a parcel over to an elderly lady,

coming around the counter to hold the door for her
with a word and a smile. Lavender dodged behind a
bolt of nankeen in order to avoid Arthur Hammond,
who had not yet seen her. She waited until Barney
was back behind the counter, then popped out from
behind the roll of material and leaned across the
work top. 'Mr Hammond!' she hissed.

Barney raised his eyebrows, looking faintly
amused. 'Miss Brabant? Is something amiss?'

Lavender frowned at him. 'Pray lean closer, sir!'

Barney obligingly bent forward. 'Yes, Miss
Brabant?'

'I have some books for you,' Lavender whispered.
'I thought you might not wish your father to see—'

Barney glanced over his shoulder at Arthur
Hammond, who was draping a roll of sarsenet around
a pillar and humming under his breath.

'Books from Northampton?' Barney whispered.
Lavender nodded, though she was not really concentrating on his words. She noticed that his eyes were
very dark brown indeed, with a ring of black around
the iris. His eyelashes were incredibly thick and
black, and his hair looked so soft and silky…

'Miss Brabant!' Barney said sharply, and
Lavender jumped, blushing.

'Yes?'

Barney looked faintly exasperated. 'I will unroll a
bolt of cambric on the counter. Slide the books beneath.'

Lavender scrabbled in her basket, gave Arthur Hammond a quick glance to ensure that he was not watching, and slid the package beneath the material.

'Thank you!' Barney gave her his heart-shaking smile. He looked over her shoulder and the smile faded. 'Not to your taste, Miss Brabant?' he asked, suddenly formal. 'Perhaps the sarsenet? There is an elegant display over by the pillar…'

Lavender sensed rather than saw Arthur Hammond standing directly behind them. She turned and threw him a dazzling smile.

'Mr Hammond! We were so very impressed by your emporium in Northampton, sir! Lady Anne Covingham was saying that it is the finest store in the whole town…' She edged towards the door, still talking, and saw to her relief that Barney had eased the books under the counter and out of sight. Arthur Hammond was preening himself and basking in her flattery, and he saw her out of the door with many fulsome compliments and thanks, totally failing to notice that Lavender had bought nothing at all.

She walked rapidly away from the shop and only paused to draw breath when she reached the Angel inn. She reflected that she was not really cut out for deception, even so simple a deception as this. It made her wonder why Barney had to hide his academic pursuits from his father, but she supposed that if Arthur Hammond was determined that his adopted son should concentrate his attentions on the shop, he might be incensed to think that Barney was distracted by other interests.

Lavender slowed her pace and paused to adjust her bonnet. It was a sunny day, but rather more humid than of late. She had forgotten her parasol again, despite Caroline's reminder.

There was the sound of running feet and Lavender turned to see Ellen Hammond hurrying down the road towards her, as she had done the day after Lavender had taken the kittens in.

'Miss Brabant!' Ellen was out of breath. 'Barney asked me to give you a message. He thanks you for bringing his books and asks if it would be possible for you to do so again when his next delivery arrives.' She blushed. 'Our father, you know, is most disapproving of Barney's studies—'

'I understand,' Lavender said quickly, wondering just what it was that Barney could be studying so secretly. She was torn, for on the one hand there was something appealing about being drawn into a conspiracy with him, even over a matter as inconsequential as some secret books. On the other, she knew it was a foolish indulgence, tempting because it would lead to further meetings... But Ellen was looking at her with such entreaty and it was impossible to resist.

'Please tell your brother that I should be only too happy if he wishes his books to be sent to Hewly,' Lavender said.

Ellen gave her a radiant smile. 'Oh thank you, Miss Brabant! You are so kind!'

They walked a little way down the road together, Ellen confiding artlessly about how hard Barney had to work and how he sometimes studied late into the night, poring over his books by candlelight. In return, Lavender told her that the kittens were growing fast on a diet of kitchen scraps provided by the indulgent servants, and that they were too lazy to catch the mice that scratched in the barn outside. She and Ellen parted company, the best of good friends, at the entrance to Perceval Hall, and Lavender watched the girl skip away up the road back into the town. Her own step was slower. There was no doubt that it would have been wiser for her to refuse Barney's request, leave well alone, avoid him… Unfortunately her own heart was now engaged and common sense had nothing to do with it.

The next consignment of books arrived ten days later. Lavender had spent the afternoon with Caroline in the garden, where her sister-in-law was advising Belton, the gardener, on the restoration project. It was Lewis and Caroline's intention to re-create the gardens of a hundred years before, when Hewly had been part of the Perceval estate. Then, as Belton never ceased to remind them, the Hewly Manor gardens had been considered amongst the finest in Northamptonshire.

It was another hot day and the sun was low as Lavender trailed back inside. She had been in the kitchen garden, where the damson, walnut and green-gage trees had provided some shade against the un-seasonably hot sun. Although she had been speaking knowledgeably of fruit trees and cold frames with Caroline and Belton, most of Lavender's mind had been preoccupied with thoughts of how and when she would contact Barney. It was Sunday on the mor-row and although they might all meet up at Abbot Quincey church, she could scarcely attend with a par-cel of books tucked under her arm.

The stone-flagged hallway of the Manor was cool in comparison with outside, and so dark that Lavender at first failed to see the figure waiting pa-tiently at the bottom of the stairs. She jumped as he stepped forward, and she saw with a little leap of the heart that it was Barney Hammond himself.

'Miss Brabant!' Barney came forward quickly, sketching her a bow. 'Forgive me for troubling you, ma'am. I was at pains to deliver your order as soon as it was ready.'

He held out a parcel that was wrapped in brown paper and tied with a ribbon. Lavender took it au-tomatically, looking a little confused.

'My order?' she echoed. 'But I did not—'

Barney shot her a warning glance. One of the maids was polishing the banisters, dusting assidu-ously as she edged ever closer to them.

'Oh, that order!' Lavender said, hoping she did not sound too hen-witted. 'How kind you are, Mr Hammond! I was not expecting it so soon!'

'Would you care to open it to see if the goods are of the appropriate quality?'

Lavender unwrapped the package hesitantly. It was a shawl, silky as gossamer and blue to match her eyes. She looked from it to Barney and saw that he was smiling.

'It is beautiful! But—'

'I wondered, perhaps,' Barney said quickly, 'whether you had anything to return to me, Miss Brabant? You mentioned that there was a fault in the cambric you purchased—'

'Oh, indeed!' Lavender said, catching his meaning. She had been puzzled by the delivery of the shawl but now saw that it was just a useful excuse. 'By chance, I was only examining that today, sir. It is indeed a pity, but I believe the consignment must be returned to you.'

'I am happy to wait if you would care to hand it back,' Barney said. 'However, if it is not convenient, perhaps…later?'

Lavender paused. Rosie was giving the banisters such a polish that Lavender feared they might wear away. She knew she could dismiss the maid so that she could talk to Barney freely, but that would only cause further speculation in the servants' hall. She could not really invite him into the drawing-room either, for that simply did not happen when the draper was delivering an order. She bit her lip. She did not like the feelings of snobbery that the whole situation engendered. In fact, it seemed all wrong for Barney to be waiting on her like this.

'If you would be good enough to call some other time, sir... I need to fetch the material and package it up, and would not care to keep you waiting...'

'I would be happy to return later,' Barney said meaningfully. 'After dinner? Perhaps we could meet as we have done before, Miss Brabant...'

Lavender walked with him to the door and watched him stroll away across the gravel sweep. She knew she had not misunderstood him. He would be waiting for her later in the woods—and she would certainly be there.

When Lavender slipped out of the gate that led from Hewly gardens to the wood that night, Barney was already standing in the shadows beneath the trees. It was just getting dark and the sky was a clear, dark blue, with the leafy outlines of the trees imprinted against it in black. Barney came forward to hold the gate open for her. Lavender could hear the brook running in the background and the wind in the trees, smell the faint, fresh scent of the forest. It was a beautiful evening.

They fell into step with each other without speaking, turning along the path that skirted the edge of the wood. Last year's leaves crunched underfoot. Lavender felt the excitement and the secrecy and the darkness stir in her blood. It was a heady mixture. She wanted to take Barney's hand and run through the wood until she was breathless.

'You have the parcel?' Barney whispered.

'Yes,' Lavender held out the brown paper package to him. 'I have also brought the shawl, as I thought—'

'That was a present,' Barney said. 'For your help, Miss Brabant.' His tone brooked no argument.

'Oh!' Lavender smiled a little diffidently. She had never received a gift from a gentleman and was not certain if she should accept. 'Well—' she tried to sound businesslike '—I have your books here! A heavy package this time! What are all these volumes that you are buying, Mr Hammond?'

Barney hesitated. 'They are works on medicine, Miss Brabant. The Northampton bookseller orders them for me from London.'

Lavender was intrigued. 'Are you then studying to be a doctor?'

Barney laughed. 'No, not that! I study pharmacy, Miss Brabant; the uses of medicaments and chemical preparations for alleviating illness. That is why I was forever in the apothecary's shop in Northampton, and why I have all these books sent to me.' He tapped the parcel under his arm. 'I am hoping that this is the new London *Pharmacopoeia,* for I have been waiting for it a while.'

'How long have you been studying these works?' Lavender enquired.

'Oh, for ever! I have some old books on botany and the healing properties of herbs…' Barney smiled. 'That was what first caught my interest, and I have always wanted to learn more of medicines and compounds.'

'Do you wish to dispense medicines—to be an apothecary yourself?'

Barney laughed again at that. 'I would rather be a pharmacist! It is the development of new cures that interests me rather than the prescribing of them! But,' his voice fell, 'I am entirely self-taught, as you may imagine, and though I have been in correspondence for a while now with a London pharmacist, it will be a long time before I can put my plans into effect! One day I aim to establish myself as a member of the Royal Pharmaceutical Society, but—'

He broke off to resume, carefully, 'Well, there is the drapery business, and my father has other ideas…' He stopped again. 'Forgive me, Miss Brabant! You have been more than kind in taking delivery of the books for me but I have no wish to bore you with my plans…'

'It is not boring,' Lavender said warmly, 'and indeed you must already know of my own interest in botany! I should be fascinated to see your old books…'

'You may borrow them if you wish,' Barney said, with a smile. 'Yes, I had not forgotten that you had been sketching the plants that day when I found you caught in the trap! And in fact I often go out collecting roots, bark and leaves, for some of my preparations. Playing truant from the shop all the time, I fear!'

'So that is why you are forever wandering in the wood—' Lavender started but stopped again hastily as she realised this was a conversational path she did not necessarily wish to follow. All her thoughts seemed to lead inevitably back to seeing him at the pool in the forest and she did not wish to speak about that. 'I thought that most cures were from plants growing in the New World rather than our own woodlands,' she said, quickly. 'Ipecac from Brazil, for instance.'

Barney slanted her a look. 'You are very well informed, Miss Brabant! Yes, it is true that a lot of our medicines were brought back by explorers and traders, but that is not to say that we cannot find our own remedies!'

'People have used herbs for generations, I suppose,' Lavender said thoughtfully. 'Nanny Pryor has a tincture she swears is sovereign against fever!'

'Exactly. I heard recently of an apothecary in Shropshire who cured dropsy with a preparation made from foxglove leaves.' Barney frowned. 'I imagine one must be careful, however. Many of these plants have poisonous effects if taken too liberally!'

'You would not wish to poison the population of Abbot Quincey in the interests of science!' Lavender said, with a giggle. 'Has anyone offered to take your preparations yet, Mr Hammond?'

'No, indeed, for I keep my work a secret!' Barney was laughing now. 'And so I cannot claim any success at all, for I have no notion whether or not they work!'

They laughed together. 'I suppose it is not just plant extracts that the apothecaries put in their mixtures,' Lavender said, after a moment. 'Do they not also use animals for their medicine? Oil of goat and grease of dog…'

'Now you are making it sound like a witch's spell,' Barney commented. 'Though it is true that some of the old remedies recommend such ingredients! I once sat by the river for hours trying to trap a heron to make a medicine that required heron's grease, but—' he shook his head '—so fastidious was I that when I netted one I was obliged to let it go at once! I could not hurt the poor creature!'

'Not even for the advancement of your science?'

'Not even for that, Miss Brabant!' Barney smiled down at her. 'Perhaps I lack the ruthlessness to be a success!'

'Success at any cost is not necessarily a victory,'

Lavender said, the smile still in her voice, 'and I cannot believe heron's grease to be truly efficacious, although I know Nanny Pryor swears by goose grease for a bad chest!'

They had reached the end of the Hewly boundary wall, having walked further than Lavender had intended. She hesitated. It had been so easy—and so pleasant—to walk with Barney in the moonlight, and the conversation had been so enjoyable that she had not wished it to end. This was strong enchantment indeed, seeing the other, more academic side to the man of action, sharing his secrets... She was aware of a strong disinclination to go back inside just yet.

'Miss Brabant...' Barney was leaning against the wall, looking at her. 'Speaking of walks in the forest, there is something that I would wish to ask you. It has been troubling me for some time, I confess.'

Lavender made a gesture of surprise. 'Then ask, sir...'

Barney hesitated. He seemed suddenly at a loss, choosing his words carefully. 'It was last June, and I had been out in the wood in the evening, collecting some plants. I was returning by the pool in the river, when I saw you down by the bank.'

Lavender stared at him. She felt suddenly cold. The breeze stirred the leaves and trickled down her spine, making her shiver.

'You were digging something out of the ground with a little trowel,' Barney continued, his gaze now riveted on her pale face. 'I believe it was the trowel you use for extracting your plant specimens. I could not see exactly what you were digging up, but it seemed to me that it was a bundle of clothes and in the moonlight they looked dark and stained… You picked them up and carried them off in the direction of home, Miss Brabant. And you were acting very furtively, looking behind you and keeping in the shadows. I confess it made me curious.' He straightened up. 'Particularly curious, since it was the day after the Marquis of Sywell had been found murdered…'

Lavender turned away sharply and gazed out across the darkening gardens. Ever since it had happened, she had been afraid of this. She had imagined herself alone that night, for she had seen no one on her hurried journey to the pool in the river. She had, as Barney had said, kept in the dark shadows and checked that no one was following her. Yet he had seen her, and for four months he had said nothing… Until now…

'Well, Miss Brabant?' Barney's voice broke into her thoughts. His tone was still low, but there was an insistent note in it. 'Am I mistaken in thinking there was a link between the murder and your strange and secretive actions? What explanation can you provide?'

'I…' Lavender cleared her throat. She did not want to lie to him, and just at the moment her mind was a total blank anyway. She could invent no story to cover what he had seen. 'It is true that I was there,' she said weakly, 'but I cannot explain to you—'

Barney shifted slightly. 'Truly? Well, if not to me then surely you could explain to the authorities investigating the case? I understand they have made precious little progress in their enquiries and might appreciate some help...'

Lavender swung round on him. 'You would not do that—'

'Would I not?' Barney raised his eyebrows. 'It's true that I had as little time for Sywell as any other man would, but murder...' He shook his head. 'Some might say that he deserved it—'

'He did deserve it!' Lavender burst out. 'You know as well as I that the man was evil—a mad, cruel despotic creature who would rape and beat and abuse indiscriminately! We are well rid of him!'

Barney sighed. 'I cannot dispute your words, but... For the sake of all those who do not sleep easy in their beds for fear of another attack—and for those on whom suspicion may fall... Miss Brabant, you must speak out!'

'I cannot!' Lavender turned away again, clenching her fists. 'I *will* not! It is not fair—'

Barney took a step closer. 'Then at least tell me who you are protecting—'

'No! I will tell nothing—'

'Is it your brother?'

Lavender swung round on him with incredulity. 'Lewis? What on earth could he have to do with this?'

Barney pulled an expressive face. 'Who knows? There are any number of candidates for the role of Sywell's murderer, are there not, Miss Brabant? The servants he abused, the villagers he ruined, the husbands he cuckolded... For all I know, Sywell might have cheated your father out of his estate after the Admiral had been struck down, and when your brother discovered it he could have threatened Sywell, and...' Barney broke off, shrugging. 'He is as good a contender as any!'

'It's nonsense!' Lavender said. Her voice was shaking now. She pressed both hands against the rough stone of the estate wall. 'You would never spread such a tale—'

'No, I would not do such a thing,' Barney conceded. 'But you must see that your actions are most suspicious, Miss Brabant! If anyone were to know...'

'It only requires for you to keep quiet!' Lavender moved closer to him, her eyes fixed on his face. 'No one else saw me—nobody knows—'

'Can you be sure of that, Miss Brabant?' Barney's tone was expressionless. 'You did not even know that I was there!'

Lavender put a hand on his arm. 'I am sure! And if I keep your secrets, surely you will keep mine!'

There was a sharp silence. Barney stared down at

her. It was too dark now to see his face, but when he spoke, Lavender thought he sounded almost amused.

'Oh Miss Brabant, what is this? Blackmail? You equate my secret studies with your desire to protect a murderer?' He stepped back, making a repudiating gesture with his hands. 'Tell, then! I'll wager it will not cause half the stir as when I tell the Lord Lieutenant that you are covering up for a murderer!'

Lavender grabbed his arm again. 'Please! You will not do that!'

'Are you concerned for yourself or for someone else?' Barney asked roughly.

'It is not like that!' Lavender screwed her face up, trying to think of a way to explain without giving away all of her secrets. 'It is just that it would cause so much trouble and misery! And no one regrets Sywell's death—'

'It is hardly your place to decide whether or not someone should be punished!' Barney said, sounding really angry now. 'You must care a great deal for him—'

'Not in the way that you mean!' Lavender faced him out. 'But I would do anything to prevent this coming out! Please—'

'Just what are you offering, Miss Brabant?' Barney's tone was suddenly smooth. 'Do you wish to stick with your blackmail, or revert to bribery instead? Your choice!'

Lavender glared at him. 'It was not my intention to bribe or blackmail! You know that!'

Barney laughed derisively. 'Do I? It seems, Miss Brabant, that I do not know you quite as well as I had imagined! But that can be remedied…'

At the last moment, and with utter amazement, Lavender realised that he was about to kiss her. She felt totally confused. She had been so wrapped up in defending herself from his accusations that it had never occurred to her that she might need to protect herself from another, more dangerous, approach. And although she had thought he was going to kiss her at the Covinghams' Ball, it had not happened and she had not really imagined that it would. She had thought of it with a little shiver of pleasure, as a forbidden extravagance. But now…

Yet for all her frightened realisation, she did not draw back from him. She felt his arm slide about her waist, pulling her against him. His hands were mercilessly hard on her slender frame, holding her still, but when his lips touched hers they were gentle, undermining her defences completely. Lavender felt her bones melt, resistance turning to response.

She had had very little experience of men, and the suitors she had met during her London season had soon bored her. Certainly she had no experience of the kind of physical awareness that Barney could evoke in her, the awareness that had been building throughout their encounter. She had never even imagined it.

When Barney let her go, the sensual excitement was still fizzing through her blood like wine. For a moment she could remember nothing of where she was, and felt disappointed and deprived that he had let her go. She put out a hand towards him and he caught it in his, pressing a kiss on the back before letting it go.

'No...' His voice was low, husky. 'Lavender, we must not. It is my fault and I am sorry—'

Lavender wanted to throw herself into his arms then and persuade him to change his mind, but Barney was already withdrawing from her, stepping back more deeply into the shadows under the trees. 'I must go. Forgive me...'

Lavender understood what he meant. She was Admiral Brabant's daughter and could not be for him, but in that moment between them, it had not mattered. This time she did not run from him, but turned and walked away slowly, deliberately. And she did not look back.

Chapter Six

Lavender lay on her back in the grass beneath the apple trees, staring through the branches at the pale blue sky. She had discarded her straw bonnet and her hair was loose about her shoulders. Instead of wearing one of her plain gowns, she had chosen a dress of dimity in pink and white stripes that was at least five years old. It was one of the ones that Julia had told her was unmodish and far too young for her, and Lavender had thrust it to the back of the wardrobe despite the fact that she liked its light, fresh colours. Now, as she lay in the orchard and contemplated the world from a different angle, Lavender wondered how she could have been so foolish as to have taken Julia's advice.

It was another Indian summer day and everyone spoke of the weather breaking with a thunderstorm. Scattered in the grass about Lavender were her crayons and drawing paper, a half-finished sketch of

Field Scabious, and her book, *Sense and Sensibility*. Lavender had started by trying to draw, found it too much effort in the heat, and had rolled over on to her stomach to read the book. As she had devoured the story of Elinor and Marianne, she had reflected that ten days ago she had compared herself to the sensible elder sister, whereas now she was set fair to throw her bonnet over the windmill like the younger one.

How had such a transformation come about? Lavender watched dreamily as the little white clouds floated across the sky. Perhaps it had been on its way for a while, or perhaps it was a sudden change. She could not be sure. After her Season in London there had been so much unhappiness—the death of her mother was followed so swiftly by that of her elder brother, and then her father's long illness... And throughout it all, Julia had been there like a sticky burr, pricking Lavender's confidence and undermining the younger girl in her own home. It was only when Lewis had come home and had married Caroline that a measure of contentment had returned.

And now...Lavender wriggled a little, a small smile curving the corners of her mouth. Now there was Barney Hammond. She had thought that he liked her and now she knew it to be true. No matter that they had quarrelled over her clumsy attempts to persuade him to keep her secret; she knew she could put that right if only she explained the whole to him.

Lavender had thought long and often about their encounter in the wood two nights before, and the memory of their kiss warmed her far more than the sun that was now beating down from a near-cloudless sky. Barney's arms about her had been reassuring and exciting at one and the same time, a promise of things to come, a remedy for unhappiness. She understood his reluctance, the thought that he was not good enough for her, and she wanted to repudiate it with all her strength. He was a fine man and she had finally come to realise that his parentage, his trade, their relative situations counted as nothing if they were truly meant for each other. She would find him and tell him so…

The warmth was soporific. Lavender's ears were full of the drowsy buzzing of the bees and she slept until the sun started to go down and the cool breeze of evening took its place. Then, shivering a little, she opened her eyes and realised that the reason she was cold was that a shadow had fallen across her. It moved, and the late afternoon sun lapped about her again.

'They said that I would find you here.'

Lavender narrowed her eyes against the reddening glare of the sun. Suddenly all she could think of was that her hair was a tumbled mess and her dress had deep creases where she had squashed it whilst reading her book. Her last coherent thought before she fell asleep had been that she would seek out Barney to tell him how she felt; his appearance at this point, before she had had time to think about her approach, was decidedly not a part of the plan.

Lavender sat up and started to pick the dried grass out of her hair. She could feel Barney's dark gaze appraising her, moving over her face and figure with an intentness that brought the colour into her already flushed face. He sat down on a nearby tree stump.

'You look very pretty today. The pink suits you.'

They were not the polished words of a society gallant but they made Lavender blush harder all the same. 'Thank you, sir. Are you… Did you wish to see me?'

'I did.' Barney looked ill at ease. His tone was suddenly formal. 'I wanted to apologise for my conduct the other night, Miss Brabant. I fear I must have given you a disgust of me—'

'Oh no!' Lavender could not help the involuntary interruption, for secretly she had hoped he would repeat his conduct plenty of times. 'Mr Hammond—'

'Please hear me out.' Barney's face was expressionless. 'Miss Brabant, I behaved towards you as no gentleman should do—'

'Please!' Lavender scrambled to her feet. 'Do not say any more, Mr Hammond!'

She realised that Barney had interpreted her embarrassment as ladylike shrinking when in fact it was simply that she did not wish to hear him humble himself. Before she could correct this false impression, he stood up.

'Yes, having said my piece I should leave you. But I would like to thank you, Miss Brabant, for your kindness in encouraging my work. I will not forget it.' He put a hand into his pocket and took out a small book. 'You mentioned that you would like to see the old books on botany that I had in my possession. This is one of them, and no use to me as I do not read the Latin script! I should be honoured if you would accept it.'

'Oh!' Lavender took the little book, feeling the smooth old leather binding beneath her fingers. 'You cannot give me this! It must be of great value—'

Barney shrugged easily. 'I inherited it from my mother but as I said, I cannot read it. I would rather it went to someone who would treasure it.' He raised an eyebrow. 'A parting gift, Miss Brabant.'

He sketched a bow and made to turn away. The tears pricked in Lavender's throat. She understood that this was a permanent farewell. What he was really saying to her was that they could not meet again—it was foolish and inappropriate to indulge in a relationship that could never lead to more. A few days before she might have agreed with him, but now she could not let him go so tamely. She thought quickly.

'Mr Hammond, if we are not to…meet again, there

is something I wish to tell you. Would you do me the honour of listening?'

Barney paused. Lavender could feel his reluctance, but she was depending on his innate good manners. Surely he would not refuse to hear her out? She held her breath.

'Very well, Miss Brabant,' Barney said unwillingly, 'but I must be gone shortly.'

Lavender gave him a smile of relief. 'Of course. Thank you! There is a bench over there beneath the trees. Shall we—'

They walked to the stone bench at the top of the orchard. Barney helped her to a seat first, then sat down an irreproachable three feet away. He did not look at her directly, but fixed his gaze a little sternly on the topiary figures that lined the path in the rose garden below. Lavender cleared her throat.

'The last time we met,' she said carefully, 'you reproached me for keeping secrets, sir. Since we will not speak like this again, there is something that I would wish you to know.'

Barney's gaze came back from the topiary and fixed on her face.

'Yes, Miss Brabant?'

'It concerns the night you saw me by the pool in the forest,' Lavender said. She took a deep breath. 'You were not mistaken, Mr Hammond. You did indeed see me dig up a bundle of clothes from a hole beneath the river bank. I brought them home and burned them on the kitchen fire.' She looked sideways at him, trying to read his face. Barney was watching her closely, but he said not one word. Somehow this seemed to make it more difficult. Lavender swallowed hard.

'It was the second time in two days that I had been to the pool,' she said slowly. 'I had been there the previous night, the night of the Marquis of Sywell's death, although I knew that not at the time. I was waiting for a night-flowering plant to bloom.' She paused, distracted. 'It was the Enchanter's Nightshade, you know, and I had heard that it opened in the moonlight, but I think it must be only a tale, for certainly I did not see it—'

'So what did you see instead?'

Barney's quietly worded question brought Lavender back to the point.

'Oh! Yes, of course. I saw a figure come down to the pool, wash himself in the water and bury something under the bank. I thought… I could not be sure…' She looked up and met his gaze. 'I could not really tell who it was.'

Barney's eyes had narrowed thoughtfully. 'But you suspect someone. I can tell—'

Lavender shivered, although the sun was still warm. She wrapped her arms about herself. 'Yes, I do suspect, but I cannot be sure. All I saw was a man's figure, though I thought I recognised him. I was mightily puzzled by what I was seeing. It was full dark, and the clothes just looked like a pile of rags. Naturally, I wondered what he was doing! But the next day I heard the tale of the Marquis's murder and I suddenly thought…'

'You thought you had seen the murderer? And you went back to the pool a second time to see what you could find?'

'I did.' Lavender pulled a face. 'Foolish of me. I should have left well alone, but curiosity…' She shrugged. 'I found the clothes hidden under the bank and they were all over blood, and so I thought that whoever it was that I had seen must have killed the Marquis that night.'

Barney was shaking his head. 'Why did you take the clothing away? And burn it! That makes you seem guilty yourself—'

'I know!' Lavender sighed. 'I sat there for what seemed like hours with the bloodstained clothes in my hands, and I thought of what would happen if I told anyone what I had seen.' She made a slight gesture. 'Oh, I did not keep quiet for scandal's sake, or anything like that, but I could not be sure of who I had seen that night and I did not want to accuse an innocent man.' She shook her head. 'I knew then that I could not tell anything of what I had seen.'

Barney shifted a little on the bench. 'But why did you burn his clothing? Why not just leave it there?'

'I was afraid that someone might stumble across it! Many people use the pool—' Lavender broke off, remembering that she had seen Barney himself swim there. 'I did not think the matter through very well,' she added hastily, 'for once the clothes were burned and gone, it suddenly occurred to me that their owner might return to retrieve them and find them missing! And I can scarce reassure him—'

Barney smiled. 'And so your deception began to catch you out! Lavender, it is clear that you know who the murderer is, or at the very least, who it was you saw that night. I would wager that you are partly keeping quiet to protect him, for all that you pretend you do not know his identity! It must be someone for whom you have a great deal of respect. Will you tell me who it was?'

Lavender shook her head. Barney's observation was perceptive, for she did indeed have a very clear suspicion of who the murderer was and she held him in the highest esteem, but even so...

'It would not be right,' she said uneasily. 'I have no wish to accuse an innocent man and I cannot be sure.' She pulled a stem of the long grass through her fingers. 'Last time we spoke of this, Mr Hammond, you told me that it was not my decision to make. Well, I have taken that right, but now you may denounce me if you wish!'

There was silence but for the soft, repetitive coo of the white doves on the Manor roof. After a long moment, Barney said, 'Why did you tell me, Miss Brabant?'

Lavender looked away from that observant regard. The truth was that it was because she loved him and could not bear him to think ill of her. The first she could not say, but perhaps the second…

'I wanted to tell you the truth,' she said, avoiding his gaze by watching the swing of the weathervane on the stables. 'I could not bear for you to believe I was protecting someone for all the wrong reasons. Nor, if I am not to see you again, could I bear you to carry away a poor opinion of me—'

'I'll not do that.' For a moment Barney's hand covered hers on the warm stone of the seat. Lavender's pulse leaped. She looked into his eyes and saw the dizzying combination of love and wanting that dried her throat and made her heart race, but in that moment it was gone and Barney was speaking again, deliberately expressionless.

'Thank you for telling me. I shall keep your secret, Miss Brabant.' Their eyes met, Barney's lightened by a faint smile. 'I shall have to trust your judgement that you are doing the right thing in keeping quiet.' He shrugged. 'Well, so be it. It has been an honour to know you, Miss Brabant, but now I must go.'

Lavender watched his tall figure walk between the trees, down the topiary path and round the side of the house to the stable yard. A few minutes later he rode out onto the drive, raising a casual hand in thanks and farewell to the groom. Lavender thought of his instinctive authority and the easy courtesy he had with all men, and raged inwardly at the barriers of birth and class that stood against him. He had recognised them himself and had bowed to the inevitable by repudiating her. And because he had done it with such grace, he had made it impossible for Lavender to oppose him.

By the time that darkness fell, the threatened thunderstorm was upon them. After dinner they sat in the library with the curtains drawn and the candles lit, and listened to the rain hurling itself against the window panes and the thunder rumbling ever closer. Lavender had abandoned the precise prose of *Sense and Sensibility* in favour of something more dashing and had plucked *Marmion* from the library shelves. Caroline was sewing and discussing developments in the American War with Lewis, who was reading them the latest dispatches as recorded in the newspaper.

'The truth is that the Americans have a navy as good, if not better, than our own,' Lewis said dryly, as he turned a page. 'I know it is hard for the Lords of the Admiralty to accept it, but those of us who served in a more humble capacity could see the change coming for many a year!' He shook his head. 'I fear that they may be in for a sharp shock!'

Lavender let her book fall to her lap and stared thoughtfully at the candles. She had fully expected to suffer a reversal of spirits after her meeting with

Barney, but was surprised to find that she felt quite buoyant. It was as though she had not really accepted that they could not be together and expected the situation to resolve itself, and soon. She did not question this rash assumption, but sat feeling content as she listened to the murmur of Lewis and Caroline's conversation, and the thunder overhead.

It was hardly a night for visitors and they all jumped when the bell sounded, harsh in the quiet house. Caroline folded her needlework into a tidy square and got to her feet.

'Gracious, who can that be calling in the middle of a storm? I know that the Covinghams said that they might call, but surely not now! Lewis—'

The door opened to admit Kimber, the butler. He bowed. 'Captain Brabant, a gentleman by the name of Sir Thomas Kenton is without. He is marooned by the storm and has stopped to seek shelter here.'

Lewis strolled out into the hall, Caroline and Lavender at his heels. An elderly gentleman was standing there, leaning on a gold-topped cane and dripping water on to the floor from his great coat. A huge flash of lightning lit the house, dimming the candlelight.

The gentleman brightened when he saw them, smiling gently and blinking with myopic blue eyes. He was frail and looked to Lavender like an elderly scholar who had unaccountably wandered out on the worst night of the year.

'Captain Brabant, sir?' The gentleman bowed to Lewis. 'Sir Thomas Kenton, at your service. Ladies…' He bowed again with old-fashioned courtesy to Lavender and Caroline, before turning back to Lewis.

'I apologise for this intrusion, sir, but I am a traveller in dire need of help and stumbled on your house through sheer good chance. Can you furnish me with the direction of the nearest inn? One of my carriage horses has gone lame and I fear I will not make home, for all that it is only ten miles—'

Lewis smiled. 'I could direct you, sir, but would not dream of turning you out into such a night as this! You must stay here, at least until the storm abates. My head groom will see to the stabling of your horses.'

Sir Thomas looked worried and relieved at the same time. 'Oh indeed, I could not thus impose on your hospitality—'

'No imposition, sir,' Caroline said now, coming forward and taking his arm. 'Kimber, pray take Sir Thomas's coat. Sir Thomas, will you take a glass of wine with us? Please join us in the library, and tell us how you come to be benighted in such a storm!'

They went back into the room, Caroline installing Sir Thomas in an armchair beside the fire, and fetching a glass of Madeira for him herself. In the light, Lavender could see that their guest was indeed frail, with a thatch of hair that was entirely white and a face as wrinkled as a walnut. Yet when he smiled he had the sweetest of expressions and a slow, warm smile that seemed strangely familiar. Lavender racked her brains, but the resemblance remained elusive.

Sir Thomas was warming his hands before the fire and reminiscing. 'I do believe it is over thirty years since I was at Hewly, or perhaps more? I forget… But it was in the days before your father bought the Manor, Captain, for I believe it was part of the Perceval estate?'

'It was indeed, sir.' Lewis smiled. 'Yet I do also believe we have met before, at one of the garden parties at Perceval Hall? It was many years ago, but you had brought a kite, your own invention, and flew it from the lawn!'

Sir Thomas looked delighted. 'Why, so I did! Yes, I recall—you were that solemn child who asked so many questions! You had an elder brother, a bucolic boy who preferred the animals, and a little sister—a pretty, fairy child with silver gilt hair…'

'I expect that that was Julia,' Lavender said.

Caroline gave her an exasperated look. 'I rather think that Sir Thomas is referring to you, Lavender!'

Sir Thomas nodded enthusiastically. 'I remember it all now! The kite became stuck in a tree and one of the Perceval children climbed up to free it and fell out and feared he had broken his leg…' He shook his head. 'Ah, fine days, fine days!'

'You were quite the inventor, sir!' Lewis said. 'I remember my father saying that you had designed the most excellent miniature battleship and that the Admiralty should have developed a full-size one!'

'Ah well,' Sir Thomas finished his wine and beamed at Caroline as she replenished his glass. 'Those days are long gone, I fear! Yet still, I have my books. I do not go into company much these days.'

'Your family?' Lavender ventured, and was sorry to see Sir Thomas shake his head sadly.

'All gone, my dear! My younger son died a long time ago, wild and foolish boy that he was.' A shadow chased away his smile. 'He had my enquiring spirit, I fear, and was forever off on mad starts! He wanted to study medicine and we quarrelled bitterly over it, for I did not see it as the work of a gentleman.' Sir Thomas shook his head again. 'Well, I was a stiff-necked old bigot in those days, but John went off abroad and fell ill with a fever and I never saw him again…'

There was a silence, but for the crackling of the fire. 'It is not good for a man to outlive his sons,' Sir Thomas said eventually. 'It makes him old to have no family about him.' He roused himself and gave them all his gentle smile. 'It is good to see new life breathed into this house, at any rate! Tell me of your plans, Mrs Brabant!'

They spent a convivial couple of hours discussing

the restoration of the house and garden, before Caroline gently pressed Sir Thomas to accept their hospitality for the night. As the rain was still drumming on the roof he took little persuasion, and presently requested a book to take up to his room with him.

'I can see I am spoilt for choice,' he said, browsing along the library shelves, and pausing to consider Plato's *Republic*. He picked it up, then put it back and took up *The Iliad* with a fond smile. 'Too martial for my time of life, perhaps… Something more soothing would be in order, I believe. Architecture, or horticulture…'

'I have a splendid book on botany here,' Lavender said, passing him the slender volume that Barney had given her earlier. 'You might not wish for the exertion of reading in Latin tonight, sir, but it is well worth the trouble! It is full of the most fascinating—'

She stopped as she saw the expression on Sir Thomas's face, a mixture of puzzlement and suspicion. He was weighing the little book in the palm of his hand and staring at it as though he had seen a ghost. He ran a hand through his thick thatch of white hair.

'Oh, but surely… This is the one that we … I thought—'

He looked from Lavender to the book, then turned a few pages.

'No mistaking…' She heard him mutter. 'The very one! And at the start—'

He turned back to the title page. 'I thought so!'

They all looked at him in confusion. 'Sir Thomas?' Caroline questioned.

Sir Thomas was holding the book up triumphantly so that the light fell on the title page. 'The arms of Kenton!' He declared. 'I thought so! This was one of my most prized works, but John borrowed it from me and I never saw it again! Of all the odd coincidences! But—' his brow furrowed '—how came it into your possession, my dear?'

'It was a present from a friend,' Lavender said hastily, seeing that Lewis and Caroline were watching her curiously. 'I saw the coat of arms, but did not know its provenance. It is of no consequence. If the book is yours, sir, then you must have it back.'

Sir Thomas looked appalled. 'My dear, I would not dream of depriving you! Your friend must surely have come by it quite honestly!' He pushed it into her hands. 'Pray keep it!'

'Oh no!' Lavender handed it back, suddenly quite desperate. 'Sir—'

'I am sure the mystery can be easily solved,' Lewis said, unwittingly making matters worse for his sister. 'Lavender, where did this come from?'

Lavender frowned at him. 'It was just a gift! Lewis, pray do not concern yourself—'

Lewis frowned in his turn. 'You are being confoundedly mysterious about this, Lavender! A gift from whom?'

'From Mr Hammond!' Lavender said, blushing. She had not wanted to confess it, for it seemed too personal to admit that Barney had been giving her presents. She tried to remember what he had said about the book's origins. 'Perhaps he bought it from the bookseller in Northampton! I cannot recall—'

'No one is suggesting that he stole it!' Caroline said mildly. 'We shall ask Mr Hammond how he came by it, and the mystery shall be solved!' She turned to Sir Thomas, who was still turning the book over in his hands. 'In the meantime, dear sir, as it is an old friend, I pray you rediscover it with pleasure! Now, is there anything else we can do for your comfort?'

Sir Thomas reassured her that he was very well served, and the party went up to bed shortly after. The storm was still rumbling in the distance, and Lavender lay awake for a while, puzzling over the botany book and its origin. Sir Thomas had said that his son had borrowed the book originally, but where it had been since, and why it had come into Barney Hammond's hands, was a complete mystery. She could remember now that Barney had told her he had inherited the book from his mother and that he could not understand the Latin text. Lavender wondered if Eliza Hammond had been able to read Latin and frowned over the mystery.

Lavender turned over and thumped the pillow into a more comfortable shape. It was cool and comforting under her cheek. It seemed too soon to seek Barney out again when he had specifically told her that they could no longer meet. Yet now she knew she would have to tell him about Sir Thomas, and ask him how a book with the arms of Kenton had ever come to be in his possession.

The following morning was overcast but warm, as though the thunderstorm had failed to lift the humidity that hung over the countryside like a blanket. Caroline sighed and claimed that her clothes were already sticking to her and that the heat made her feel indisposed. Lavender resolved to take refuge in the woods with her sketching paper until she had decided when she dared to approach Barney again.

They were still at breakfast when they heard the sound of a carriage on the drive and the knocker sound a moment later. Fluting female tones wafted on the air. Caroline and Lavender exchanged a look.

'More visitors!' Caroline said, with a lift of her brows. 'How diverting! Here we are going along with our own company all this time, then suddenly—'

'That sounds like—' Lavender began, then the breakfast-room door swung open, and Julia Chessford stood on the threshold, exquisitely bridal in a cream satin dress and matching lace-adorned cape.

'My dears!' She held her arms wide and for a dreadful moment Lavender wondered if she were about to embrace them all. 'I promised that I would visit, did I not, and here I am!'

Lavender noticed that Lewis seemed to be having trouble keeping his face straight. 'So you did, Julia,' he murmured, 'but I am not at all sure that we believed you!'

Given that Mrs Chessford had left the Manor under something of a cloud previously, it seemed odd to Lavender that she had had the impertinence to return and expect a welcome. It was also unfortunate that Sir Thomas Kenton was an unwitting spectator to the scene, since it made it impossible for Lewis to suggest that his cousin turn round and depart the house directly. In short order, therefore, Julia had drawn a chair up to the breakfast table and had prettily requested that the maid bring her some food: 'Eggs buttered just as I like them, Rosie, and a cup of chocolate—not too sweet, not too bitter…'

Caroline caught Lavender's eye and grimaced at her. Her lips formed the words 'pockets to let.' Lavender nodded slightly. They both suspected that it could not be a fondness for their company that had led Mrs Chessford to take refuge at Hewly, but the fact that she was an inveterate gambler and was probably without a feather to fly. Lavender sighed and

toyed with her food. Julia's arrival had acted to sup-
press the appetite and much else too. Just now she
was expressing naïve surprise that Lewis and
Caroline had yet to redecorate the house, which had
been shabby even when she had last been there. She
then turned her most dazzling smile on Sir Thomas,
and quizzed the unsuspecting baronet about his estate
and fortune. Sir Thomas answered her with the same
mild courtesy that he had shown previously, evidently having little suspicion that he was being sized
up as a potential husband.

'Is she not shameless!' Caroline said later, having
grabbed Lavender's arm and practically dragged her
from the breakfast-room. She wiped the tears of
laughter from her eyes. 'I suspect that Julia has lost
her beau and that poor Sir Thomas is being considered as a replacement!'

Lavender's shoulders shook. 'No doubt she would
think him ideal—elderly, rich and childless! Oh dear,
Caro—should we have left the poor gentleman alone
with her? They will be betrothed ere breakfast is
over!'

Sir Thomas, however, proved surprisingly resilient
to Julia's charms. When they ventured back into the
room they found him in the middle of a discourse on
agricultural improvements at Kenton, and he explained that his charming companion had been asking him about his interests. Julia was hiding her
yawns behind one white hand and angling for a visit

to Kenton Hall, but in vain. Sir Thomas promised to send her a tract on land reform, thanked Caroline gravely for her hospitality and stated that he must be on his way home. He kissed Lavender's hand with old-fashioned gallantry.

'Thank you for the loan of your botanical book, my dear,' he said with a twinkle in his eye. 'I enjoyed rediscovering such a treasure! Now it is yours and I hope it brings you pleasure! And if you wish to study the rest of my library, you shall be very welcome at Kenton Hall!'

Julia pouted as the door closed behind him. 'What a prosy old bore! And what a waste! Why, I declare, that estate is worth ten thousand a year and it will all go to some distant nephew on Sir Thomas's death! Lud, if I could attach his interest—'

'I should concentrate on the distant nephew, Julia,' Caroline advised, sitting down and pouring herself another cup of chocolate from the pot. 'He will be younger and may be more susceptible to your charms! I fear Sir Thomas is only interested in his land and his books—a shame, but you could never compete with Plato!'

Julia brightened. 'Oh, a capital idea, Caro! I shall make enquiries! Now, how do the two of you plan to entertain me today?'

Caroline tried and failed to look apologetic. 'I fear the heat makes me feel quite enervated, Julia, so I shall be resting in my room! Lavender?'

Lavender smiled. 'I am working on my botanical collection today, cousin Julia! If you wish to accompany me into the wood, you are very welcome!'

Julia gave a little shudder. 'Lud, how unpleasant! The heat and the flies...' Her blue eyes sharpened spitefully. 'It amazes me that you are still devoting yourself to that boring old study, Lavender! Still, when a lady has no prospect of marriage and family, I suppose it is good to have a hobby! I shall drive into Abbot Quincey, I think, and call on the Percevals. I have no doubt they will be delighted to see me again!'

Lavender and Caroline exchanged a look. Both remembered that when Julia had last tried calling on their aristocratic neighbours, most of them were unaccountably from home.

'Just as you wish, Julia,' Caroline murmured. She turned to Lavender. 'Do not tire yourself out walking, my love. This heat is very intense. And be careful where you go. I know you think the forest is safe, but I have had enough strange experiences in there to make me know that it is anything but!'

Chapter Seven

It was a hot afternoon. Lavender struggled across the meadow with her portfolio of sketches clutched under one arm and her skirts held up in the other hand. She could feel the material of her dress sticking to her back in the sunshine and wished that she had worn something lighter. One did not expect such warmth in early October.

She had spent the morning drawing plants for her collection and now, by mid-afternoon, felt sleepy and ill-disposed to do any more work. On the other hand she felt disinclined to return to the Manor, where Julia was no doubt well settled in by now and busy stirring up trouble.

She wandered towards the river, drawn by the cool sound of the water playing over the stones. Here under the trees it was shady, but the air was still humid. Lavender propped her portfolio against a tree trunk and made her way towards Steepwood Pool. She was feeling a strong desire to plunge into the water fully clothed, but her natural modesty prevented her from swimming there, no matter how refreshing it might be. She decided that she would make do with bathing her hands and face, and she unfastened the buttons at the neck of her gown so that she could feel the breeze against her hot skin.

As she drew near to the water, Lavender could see that the pool was already occupied. Someone else had had the same idea as she, only they had no qualms about stripping off for a quick dip in the water. She knew that she should not linger, but she stood watching for a split second, a second too long.

As she hesitated, she saw the figure reach the bank and pull himself out of the water. It was Barney Hammond. There was no mistaking that broad, well-made figure, the dark hair glistening now with droplets of water. He was naked from the waist up, barefoot, and his soaking trousers clung to his muscular legs. Lavender saw him raise his hands to rub the water from his face, and she caught her breath as the hazy light burnished his skin from golden to deep bronze. Her heart was racing and a peculiar excitement lit her blood, the same feeling as when he had kissed her that time, an undercurrent of sensuous pleasure. Lavender stared, and Barney raised his head and looked directly at her.

In that moment Lavender was suddenly reminded of all the respectable reasons why she should not lurk in the forest spying on semi-naked men. She turned away hastily and started to walk back to pick up her portfolio, but even as she retreated she was aware that he was following her. Her skirts were long and the forest floor strewn with branches and brambles to trap the unwary. Barney reached her in what seemed to Lavender only half a dozen easy strides, caught her arm and pulled her round to face him with negligent ease.

'Miss Brabant!' He did not even sound out of breath. 'Why are you running away?'

It was more a challenge than a question. Lavender raised her chin.

'I was *walking* away, sir, because I had understood that you did not wish to meet with me any more and besides,' she could not help herself from looking at him pointedly, 'you are scarce in a fit state to greet a lady!'

Barney glanced down at the breeches that were still moulded to his thighs and grinned.

'You have not let that weigh with you before, ma'am, on the other occasions when you have watched me in the forest or at the pool!'

Lavender opened her mouth to deny it and closed it again. The colour flooded into her face. She could hardly deny that she had seen him fencing with James Oliver, and as for the rest... She had always suspected that he knew she had seen him at the pool before. And it was so undignified for a lady to be caught spying.

'I... I beg your pardon, sir,' she managed to force out. 'It was never my intention to...to deliberately watch you—'

Barney raised his eyebrows in a gesture that conveyed disbelief more clearly than any words.

'Indeed?' he drawled. 'Well, if you were only intending to take a swim yourself, why do you not do so?' He gestured behind him. 'There is plenty of room for two!'

Lavender's eyes opened wide. 'Oh, I could not! It would not be seemly—'

'Less seemly than to watch in secret?' Barney questioned. He was smiling slightly. 'You have an odd idea of proper behaviour, Miss Brabant!'

Lavender bit her lip. It seemed he was not going to let her off lightly. 'I told you that it was an accident, sir—'

'Oh, so you did—'

'One meets many people and sees many things in the forest!' Lavender burst out, stung by his sarcasm.

Barney grinned, his teeth very white in his dark face. He leant one hand against the trunk of the nearest tree. Lavender fixed her gaze on the distant stands of oak and ash. She knew he was watching her but she could not look him in the eye. She certainly did not want to look lower, where his bare torso still gleamed with stray drops of water, or lower even than that where his damp trousers outlined his body with all the explicit beauty of a classical statue.

'I must go,' she said. 'It is too hot to be wandering out here—'

It was true. The air around them seemed to shimmer with a heavy, sensual heat.

'I see that you had already started to unfasten your dress,' Barney said expressionlessly, his gaze lingering on the hollow in Lavender's throat, where she knew a frantic pulse was now beating. 'Are you sure that I cannot tempt you into the pool?'

Lavender felt suffocated. What she wanted and what she knew she should do were now drifting ever farther apart. She cleared her throat. 'No, truly, I should go—'

Her words sounded weak even to her own ears and Barney ignored them, straightening up and stepping closer to her.

'Then at least take off your straw bonnet. There is no direct sunlight here and it would be far more pleasant for you to feel the air on your face…'

He put out a hand and took hold of the end of one of her ribbons, pulling gently until the bow unravelled. Lavender could feel the bonnet slipping back and tumbling to the ground. It was true—there was the very slightest of breezes that day, and it was warm on her hot face.

She had tied her hair in a plait that morning and pinned it up, and now she saw Barney's hand move again and the sunlight glinted on the golden heads of the pins as he methodically pulled them out. She could feel his fingers in her hair, feel the slippery weight of it gather and start to fall about her shoulders. Neither of them said anything.

Barney gathered a handful of the silver gilt threads and let them slip between his fingers. 'That's better. I wanted to see it like this again. You looked so beautiful yesterday lying in the grass with your hair spread about you—'

'You should not…' Lavender's words came out as a whisper. She was trembling all over, afraid that her legs were about to give way. She knew her breathing was quick and shallow and she could not tear her gaze away from him for fear—and fascination—of what he would do next.

Barney brushed the long strands of hair away from her neck, his fingers just grazing her skin where the collar of her dress was open. When he started to undo the tiny pearl buttons down the bodice, Lavender felt her trembling increase. Her throat was dry but her skin felt flushed and sticky with sweat. She felt light-headed and more than a little faint, and she could think of nothing but that she wished Barney would kiss her, and that there was the most intolerable ache inside her and that she would do anything she could to appease it.

There was a look of intense concentration on Barney's face as his hand drifted lower, undoing another button, a second, a third… His gaze fell to where the edge of Lavender's white lawn shift was now visible, with the slight curve of her breasts above.

Lavender made a slight noise, half-gasp, half-moan, and put a hand out, but whether to stop the progress of his fingers or to help him, she did not know. In the event he captured her hand and returned it to her side, the same look of distilled concentration on his face. Her back was against a tree; she felt its rough bark against her palms as she steadied herself. Barney had unfastened the buttons almost to her waist now and was sliding the material of her bodice over her shoulders so that the dress crumpled to her feet and she stood in her shift alone. Lavender, who had ten minutes before contemplated and rejected the idea of stripping down to just such a state of undress for her swim in the pool, shivered convulsively at what she was discovering.

She longed to touch him. The proximity of that hard, tanned body to hers was almost too much to bear, and she reached for him again, gasping with relief this time as he pulled her into his arms.

His voice was so soft she could hardly hear it. 'Oh, Lavender… I have so wanted this…'

Lavender wanted it too. As his mouth took hers at last she closed her eyes, abandoning herself to touch and taste.

The kiss was almost violent with pent-up emotion.

Lavender's lips parted, responding wildly to the demand of his. Sensuality flared between them, a scalding tide in Lavender's blood. She pressed closer to him, running her hands over the muscles of his bare back and revelling in the groan she wrung from him with her caress. His skin was smooth and cool, still slightly damp from the water. Barney kissed her again, fiercely, hungrily, tilting her chin up so his mouth could plunder the sweetness of hers. His lips moved to the corner of her mouth, then to the sweet hollow of her throat, then down… Lavender arched against him, in an agony of wanting until she felt his fingers cup her breasts through the thin shift, felt him push the material aside and lower his head to take one sensitive tip in his mouth. A dart of exquisite pleasure shot through her. His stubble grazed her exposed skin and she gasped aloud.

They tumbled down into the grasses and lay there, winded, adrift with desire, and only inches apart.

Lavender opened her eyes. She was lying on her back staring up at the pattern of green leaves against a pale blue sky. Barney was propped on his elbow beside her, still watching her with that intent, concentrated desire. She could see the tiny, golden hairs on his forearm, and put out one finger and ran it along his arm. He was warm to touch and smelled of sunshine and fresh air. Barney smiled, a slow, lazy smile that made her quiver. He pulled her back into his arms, sliding one hand inside her unlaced shift, his fingers teasing her breasts again. Lavender's head fell back, her hair spread about her.

'Kiss me again…'

She heard Barney laugh. His voice was very husky. 'Are you sure that's what you want, Lavender?' He leant over her, kissing the soft skin of her breasts. 'More than this…'

Lavender's voice caught on a sigh as she closed her eyes. 'Oh…'

He was kissing her again, they were tangled in each other's arms, blind to all else, deaf to intrusion. It was only when a heron rose flapping mightily from the pond and scared all the other birds out of the trees, that Lavender stirred and pulled a little away.

'Barney? Was someone there?'

The mood was broken. They sat up. They could see no one between the ranks of dark trees, but Lavender shivered a little. Her gaze went to her disordered clothing and she drew her shift together with shaking fingers. Her mind was numb—she could not regret what she had done, nor even think about it clearly. All she knew was that she had wanted Barney to make love to her, wanted it to the exclusion of all else, but that now the moment had gone.

The air was still hot and heavy, humming with bees, but now it felt more like the prelude to another thunderstorm. Lavender picked up her dress and struggled to do up all the little buttons.

Barney had been watching her, his expression inscrutable. Now he got up and came across to her. She knew he could see how much she was still trembling, how her hands shook on the buttons.

'Here, let me.' He spoke quietly, buttoning them up with as much swift efficiency as he had used in unfastening them. He finished and stood back a pace.

'Lavender—'

Lavender suddenly realised that she was about to cry. She did not know why, only that her throat was closed with tears that threatened to spill over.

'Please, don't—'

'Sweetheart…' Barney ignored her plea and the stiffness of her body to take her in his arms, and after a moment she relaxed. He spoke into her hair.

'Lavender, after the last time I kissed you I swore to myself that it would not happen again.' He held her a little away from him, touching one hand gently to her cheek. 'I apologised then, but I was not sorry and nor am I now. Given a choice…' He shook his head slowly. 'But there is no choice. We cannot meet again.'

Lavender looked up, her drenched lavender-blue eyes suddenly furious. 'You are scarcely gallant in your rejection! After all that has just happened between us—'

Barney let go of her. 'You know it is not like that… I could wish for nothing more than you, but it cannot be.' A look of exasperation came over his features. 'Oh Lavender, be sensible! There cannot be anything between us—'

'It is a little late in the day for that!' Lavender lifted her chin defiantly. 'I wish you had not stopped—at least then you might act as a gentleman ought!'

There was a closed look on Barney's face. 'I am no gentleman and you know that that is precisely the problem! I have nothing to offer you, Lavender! I wish it were otherwise, but it is not!'

Lavender came close to him, resting both hands against his bare chest. 'But you want me—you know it…'

There was a tight, strained look on Barney's face. 'It is not that simple—'

'Why not?' A huge knot of jealousy had formed in Lavender's chest. She banged her clenched fist against his arm. 'Why with all those other girls— village girls to be tumbled as you please—and not me?'

Barney caught her wrist. 'In the first place, there were no other girls! And in the second, even had there been, you are not like them!'

Lavender was silenced by his first statement, rather than by the obvious truth of the second. She stared. 'No other girls? What—never?'

'No.'

'But surely…' Lavender hesitated. 'They are forever throwing themselves at you! And…and it was clear that you knew what you were about…'

She saw Barney smile as he bent to retrieve her bonnet from the long grass. 'I am flattered that you should think so! In fact I think we were both about to find out for the first time!' He shot her a look. 'What do you take me for, Lavender? Yes, it is true that I have had offers, but why should I avail myself of them?'

Lavender frowned. 'I just… I suppose I thought… It is the way of the world!'

Barney shrugged. 'That may be so, but it is not my way.' A shade of colour stole into his face. 'I wanted to wait until I had found something better, and the irony is that I have now found it, but I cannot take it!' He looked at her angrily. 'This is pointless! I am sorry, but it cannot be. Now, please excuse me. I must go.'

Lavender put out a hand to stop him, but he shook her off and turned away.

'No, Lavender! Do not, I beg you, try my self-control any further!'

Lavender watched him walk firmly away from her, back to the edge of the pond where he retrieved his shirt and pulled it on. He did not look her way again. Presently, when he had put his boots back on and picked up his jacket, she saw him walk back towards the path that led to Abbot Quincey. He did not spare her another glance, merely walking, head bent, and resolutely avoiding her gaze. She watched him until he disappeared through the trees, then she started to walk slowly back in the direction of Hewly. Her portfolio was still propped against the tree where she had left it, what seemed like hours before.

She picked it up and wandered back towards the house, still trying to sort out her thoughts and feelings. She felt warm and dazed, happy and sad, all mixed up together. She knew now that she loved Barney deeply and, from all the things that he had said, she was certain he loved her too. He had claimed himself to be no gentleman but as far as Lavender could see, his reticence to press his suit was for very chivalrous reasons. He felt that he had nothing to offer her and whilst she, dazzled and bewildered by her emotions, might consider that she would be happy living in a cottage with him, he was evidently thinking of what was due to an Admiral's daughter, a lady descended from two very distinguished families.

Lavender smiled a little to herself, swinging her bonnet by its ribbons. The material point was surely that Barney cared for her, and since that was the case, she would persuade him to change his mind. She had not the least notion how she would accomplish this, but she was very determined. She knew she would prevail. She was so wrapped up with her newly discovered emotions that not even Julia's sharp asides could trouble her, and she spent the rest of the day floating around the house with a faint smile on her lips and a dreamy look in her eyes.

It was still early the following morning when there was a tumultuous rapping at the door followed by the sound of a decided altercation in the hall outside. Kimber trod into the room looking very slightly ruffled.

'Excuse me, Captain Brabant. There is a person here demanding to see you. He says that it is very urgent. I have taken the liberty of showing him into your library, sir. It is Mr Arthur Hammond—'

Lavender turned her head sharply, dropping her piece of toast on to the floor where it was immediately attacked by one of the kittens. Her reaction was not lost on Julia, whose blue eyes sharpened with interest. Lewis put down his napkin with a look of resignation and got to his feet.

'Very well, Kimber, thank you. We seem to be plagued with early morning visits at the moment! Ladies—' He dropped a kiss on Caroline's head '—pray excuse me!'

'Whatever can that be all about!' Caroline said, pouring herself another cup of tea. 'Arthur Hammond, and so early in the morning! I am sure that we have paid all our bills most promptly!'

Julia's big blue eyes moved from Caroline's face to Lavender's flushed one. 'I may be mistaken,' she said with a hint of malice, 'but I believe that Cousin

Lavender may know the answer to that one! Lavender? What do you have to say, my dear?'

Lavender knew that she was blushing even more. She hated Julia's spiteful ways. 'I fear I have no notion what you mean, Cousin Julia,' she said with as much composure as she could muster. 'The matter is no doubt being resolved between my brother and Mr Hammond as we speak—'

It seemed, however, that she had spoken too soon. Despite the fact that the study was across the hall and that both doors were doubtless closed, the sound of a voice raised in strident emotion, could now be heard.

'Captain Brabant, if you wish your sister's good name to be bandied about the villages like a common strumpet—'

Caroline stood up, gently putting the other kitten down on the carpet. She cleared her throat. 'Well, I think I shall rest for a little. I feel fatigued again this morning. Lavender, will you come up with me and read to me?'

They were too late to escape, however. As they went out into the hall, Arthur Hammond's voice, even louder and disastrously clear even from behind the study door, could be heard bellowing, 'The rumours are all over the village, sir! Either they announce their engagement immediately or Miss Brabant is ruined!'

Caroline shot Lavender a quick glance and moved

closer to her side as the study door opened and Lewis propelled Hammond out into the hall, evidently intending to throw him out of the house. Behind them, Julia stood in the breakfast-room doorway, her face registering excitement and spite. Lavender felt sick.

Hammond had not stopped talking even whilst he was being manhandled towards the door. His voice had sunk a little now, become ingratiating.

'Come now, it is not so bad a match, Captain! Your little sister may have the breeding but my boy has the money! Or at least he could have if I chose to be generous, and with such a match I could be more than that—'

Lewis's voice interrupted him, cold and cutting.

'Mr Hammond, I do not think that that is in the least pertinent to the situation! I shall speak to no one but your son about this! If he wishes to come here and explain why he has compromised my sister's good name—'

'My son knows nothing of this!' Hammond sounded pugnacious. His embroidered waistcoat swelled alarmingly. 'It is I who have come here, as a good father should, to try to save the reputations of my son and your sister, Captain Brabant! Your refusal to discuss the matter seriously—'

'Believe me, Hammond, I take the matter very seriously indeed!' There was a glitter in Lewis's eye and his mouth was drawn into a tight line, suggesting a temper barely held under control. Lavender saw his gaze sweep over them, lingering with contempt on Julia's avid little face. 'However, I will discuss this only with your son, and certainly not within earshot of my guests and my servants!'

'Very commendable, Captain,' Hammond sneered. 'Your servants are at this very moment discussing the gossip they have already heard in Abbot Quincey—'

'Doubtless,' Lewis said coldly. ''I must ask you to leave now, Hammond. At the moment there is nothing further for us to consider. Kimber, show the gentleman out!'

Hammond looked somewhat nonplussed. Kimber, his face as wooden as a church pew, held the front door open.

'Good day, sir,' he said, in sepulchral tones.

Hammond, still blustering, was expelled on to the gravel sweep before the front door. Inside the hall there was a charged silence.

'Lavender,' Lewis said, very politely, 'I wonder if you would be so good as to join me in the study?'

Caroline suddenly woke up to the fact that Julia was lapping the scene up. 'Julia!' She grabbed their cousin's arm. 'Would you care to give me your opinion on the new red damask for the dining-room? You are such an arbiter of taste!' And she positively hauled a reluctant Mrs Chessford away.

Lewis stood aside courteously for his sister to precede him into the study. Lavender's heart was beating light and fast. She so seldom saw Lewis angry, for he had the most equable nature, but when his temper was really aroused it could be fearsome. Since he had returned from sea the previous year, they had built up a strong friendship and she could not bear to lose his good opinion. She locked her hands together to still their trembling, and eyed him nervously. Lewis strolled over to the window.

'Do sit down, Lavender. Or remain standing, if you prefer.' He gave her the ghost of a smile. 'It is sometimes easier to face difficult situations on your feet!'

Lavender smiled back a little tremulously. Lewis's gaze searched her face. 'Would you care for a drink? Something reviving?'

Lavender shook her head. 'No, thank you, Lewis. What did Mr Hammond have to say?'

Lewis grimaced. 'Arthur Hammond tells me—and indeed the whole household!—that there are rumours circulating in Abbot Quincey. Rumours that link you with his son. No doubt you heard most of what he had to say.' Lewis drove his hands into his pockets. 'Apparently you were seen at Steepwood Pool yesterday, Lavender, in a somewhat…intimate situation—'

He broke off as Lavender blushed bright red and pressed both her palms to her cheeks. She took an involuntary step back.

'Oh, no! There was someone there! I wondered at the time—'

Lewis raised his brows. He looked ever so slightly taken aback. 'Are you telling me that the rumour is true, then?'

Lavender met his eyes and looked quickly away. 'Yes… No! I suppose,' she looked away, 'it must have looked bad…'

Lewis walked back to the centre of the room. 'Would you consider your reputation to be compromised?' he asked in measured tones. 'Forgive me, Lavender, I have no wish to cause you further distress, but—'

Lavender burst into tears. 'Oh, I suppose so! Yes, I can see that people might consider it so… He said that he had nothing to offer me, and I know he was only trying to be noble but I love him…'

Lewis did not say another word, but came across and took her in his arms. Lavender cried into his shoulder.

'Oh Lewis, it is not *fair*—'

'I know,' her brother stroked her hair gently. 'But Lavender, he is right—'

'I don't care!' Lavender wept harder. 'I would marry him tomorrow—'

Lewis was shaking his head, but he did not say anything further and in a little Lavender's sobs quietened. Her heart felt weighted with lead. She knew that from any worldly point of view, both Lewis and

Barney were right. He did not have anything to offer her and the match would be the most unequal imaginable. Yet that did not matter to her, not when she wanted to spend the rest of her life with him. And now that everyone was talking…

'What happens now?' she asked forlornly, reaching for her handkerchief to try to mop her face.

Lewis passed her his. 'I think we need to hear what Mr Hammond has to say. He may well feel that he cannot marry you, but he has damaged your reputation—'

Lavender's eyes filled with tears again.

'It is not his fault!'

'But he must take that responsibility!' Lewis moved a little away. 'Lavender—'

There was a sharp rat-a-tat at the front door. 'If that is Arthur Hammond back with his latest set of demands, I shall have him horsewhipped from the house!' Lewis said feelingly.

Lavender, for all her misery, stifled a giggle. 'Oh dear, to contemplate such a father-in-law…'

Lewis looked bleak. 'Let us not contemplate any such thing until we have considered all possibilities! Now—'

'Begging your pardon, sir.' Kimber, even more expressionless than before, was in the doorway. 'Mr Barnabas Hammond is here and asking for an immediate interview.'

'How timely!' Lewis said dryly. 'Show him in, Kimber!'

Chapter Eight

Lavender had no particular desire for Barney to see her in such a state of dishevelment and tried to edge out of the study before he came in, but Lewis prevented her from doing so by catching hold of her hand and refusing to let go.

'You will have to face him at some point,' he said in an undertone. 'See what the poor fellow has to say first before you run away!'

Lavender gave him a shaky smile. 'I am no coward—I will not run away! But Lewis, I need time to think—'

Her brother nodded. 'You will have all the time you need, Lavender, but hear Mr Hammond out first—'

He broke off as Barney came in and though he let go of Lavender's hand he did not move far away. Lavender found this comforting. It seemed that no matter how deep her disgrace, neither Lewis nor Caroline was going to abandon her.

Barney came into the room with a firm tread but his confidence was belied by the distraught look on his face. He was white and strained and he addressed himself directly to Lewis.

'I beg your pardon for intruding in this manner, Captain Brabant! I know it must seem most singular, but my business is urgent!' His gaze flickered to Lavender for the first time. 'If I could see you alone—'

'Certainly,' Lewis said, with suspicious alacrity. 'I imagine that you will then wish to speak with my sister, Mr Hammond?'

'I…yes…' Barney's gaze went back to Lavender again and she could have sworn that it softened as it rested on her. 'Miss Brabant, I beg your pardon…'

'There is nothing to apologise for, sir,' Lavender said tremulously, and saw him smile a little, a smile edged with sadness. She turned to Lewis. 'I shall wait in the library.'

Lewis nodded, giving her an encouraging smile of his own, and she went out of the room and closed the door gently behind her.

The house was quiet. Caroline had evidently managed to keep Julia locked away somewhere and the servants had all retreated behind the green baize door. Lavender went into the library and curled up in a window-seat.

She could feel all the happiness of the day before slipping away, oozing out of her like the stuffing from a cushion. She wondered if perhaps she had imagined that she and Barney could have a chance of happiness, and had been deluding herself that she could persuade him to overlook the inequalities of their relative social positions. Now that matters had come to a head, it seemed that that was all anyone could think of.

Lavender sighed. Whilst it might be an accepted thing for a man to marry beneath him, particularly for fortune, the same could not be said of a lady. She understood what Lewis had been implying, knew that in the eyes of the world she would be making a deplorable *mésalliance*. And yesterday Barney had been adamant that he would never ask her to do so. Now, however, his hand had been forced…

She was not sure how long she had been sitting there when the door opened and Barney came in. He was still very pale under his tan and his expression was set. Lavender got to her feet, suddenly nervous. Barney came across to her and took one of her cold hands in his.

'Miss Brabant. Yesterday I explained why I could not offer for you despite the esteem in which I hold you. It now seems, however, that I have compromised your reputation and I accept that that is true and that I must take the blame for it. I therefore have your brother's permission to ask for your hand in marriage.' He stepped back punctiliously, releasing her.

'You would do me great honour—the greatest honour—in accepting my offer.'

Lavender took a deep breath. His words had hurt her, for he made no bones about the fact that he was only proposing out of necessity. This was not how she had wanted it, and it seemed so cruel that she had had no time to talk him round, to change his mind…

She tried to smile.

'Pray, sir, may we not sit down and discuss this in a comfortable way? I fear that all this emotion so soon after breakfast will overpower me!'

Barney gave her a slight smile, but he sat down beside her on the window-seat and she saw him relax a little. He took her hand again, this time more naturally.

'Lavender, I am sorry that this is not as you would have wished it! God knows, I hold you in the highest esteem and could wish for nothing more than that you would be my wife! But,' he shook his head, 'I must ask you to also to consider the change in your circumstances, were you to marry me.' He got to his feet again restlessly, as though he was unable to stand the thoughts that crowded in on him, and took a few agitated paces away from her before turning back with a gesture of despair.

'I feel sick at heart to be asking this of you! How

long would it be before you regretted so hasty a marriage? You might become bitter and resentful, longing for what you had given up!'

He saw her instinctive gesture of denial and hurried on. 'Oh, you say now that you would never feel like that, but what can I offer you? I do not even have a profession! What, are you to live above the draper's shop? You, a lady brought up here at the Manor? Are you to help me serve behind the counter, dealing with the customers, at my father's beck and call?' He turned violently away from her. 'It is intolerable! And yet that is what I am asking of you, because now I am obliged to offer you the protection of my name—and that is all I can offer you! No home, no profession, nothing of my own!'

Lavender put her hands over her ears. 'Barney, I shall not listen! It need not be like that—'

'That is precisely how it is!' Barney's eyes were black with fury now. Lavender dimly realised that his anger was not for her, but for the frustration and cruelty of their situation. She stood up, moved across to him.

'Barney, listen. It is not as you suggest—'

'In fact it is even worse than I am suggesting!' Barney's face was tight with self-loathing. 'You may not know that I am no son of Hammond's, only his bastard nephew! I hold the little that I do have from his charity! I do not even have a name of my own to offer you! And you—' He closed his eyes briefly,

to open them again and focus intensely on her face.
'You have a considerable fortune of your own, not a
penny of which would I touch if we married—'

'Barney, stop!' Lavender came close to him, compelling his attention with her eyes. She put both her
hands on his arms, holding him still.

'I would feel my fortune had been put to a noble
use if it enabled you to pursue your ambition—'

Barney broke away from her. 'No! It is all wrong!'

'That is just foolish pride talking—' Lavender
took a deep breath and spoke more calmly. 'You
have done *me* the honour to ask me to be your wife.
I am fully aware of the…disadvantages you perceive
in our situation, but…' she kept her eyes fixed on his
face '…I love you.'

She slid her hands up to his shoulders and stood
on tiptoe to kiss him. After a moment she felt his
arms go round her and he bent his head to hers. The
kiss was deep and sweet, but there was an edge of
desperation to it and after a moment Barney freed
himself. There was despair in his face.

'Lavender, I love you too, but it is not enough…'

Lavender stood back out of the circle of his arms.
She felt suddenly cold. Her gaze scoured his face and
a part of her withered at what she saw there. She
spoke slowly.

'Very well, then, Mr Hammond. If that is the case,
I cannot marry you. You give with one hand, then
take away. You offer me marriage, then tell me all

the reasons why I should not accept! I love you and you say that you love me too, yet that is not enough for you. Well, I am braver than you. It would have been enough for me. But have no fear. I will not accept you. I thank you for the honour that you have done me, but I fear I must decline your offer.'

It was when she saw the relief in his face, fleeting as it was, that her heart truly broke. She was not sure how she kept her composure long enough to dismiss him, but her voice did not even shake.

'There is nothing more to say. Good day, Mr Hammond.'

When she heard the door close behind him, she threw herself down on the window-seat again and cried and cried.

'It is very difficult,' Caroline said, with what her sister-in-law thought was huge understatement. 'On the one hand, Mr Hammond is in the right of it, for there is no doubt that it would be a very unequal match in worldly terms!'

Lavender took a turn about her bedroom. She had locked herself away earlier, wanting to see no one, but Caroline had persuaded her to let her in and was now sitting curled up on the end of Lavender's bed.

'Why does everyone have to think in such a way?' Lavender demanded. Her head ached from the misery of it all. 'Barney is in every way my equal—he is clever and compassionate and kind, yet no one rates those qualities and everyone thinks only of money and position—'

'Here's a pother!' Caroline said, eyes twinkling. 'You have no need to defend him to me, Lavender! I like Barney Hammond immensely and it has not escaped my notice that he is all the things you say and a very attractive man into the bargain! But—' the light died from her eyes '—there is no doubt that if you marry him you will be making what the world views to be a huge mistake. Further, there is a practical point. You may think now that you could tolerate any circumstance for love, but in practice I think you would find it difficult. Leaving aside the slights and sneers of your fellow men, you would have that pushing Arthur Hammond as a father-in-law and a husband who was obliged to work in a shop. Surely you can see that your circumstances would not be enviable!'

Lavender went over to the window and stared out into the dusk. Suddenly she wanted to escape the house, escape the intolerable problem of her future. The picture that Caroline had painted was bleak indeed and she could not deny it. It would have taken a great deal of love and tenacity to overcome it. She had been prepared to take a risk on that love, but Barney had not—and that was the end of it. So perhaps, after all, there was no debate.

Briefly Lavender thought of Barney's secret plans to study to become a pharmacist. She could have funded his studies if he had been prepared to swallow his pride and accept her money. They could have been free of Hammond's influence, they could have been happy…

But Barney had shown himself too stubborn to agree to live off his wife's charity, even for love. Lavender pressed her head against the cool window-panes and closed her eyes for a moment.

She turned back restlessly to Caroline.

'There is another alternative, although we have not yet spoken of it. I have refused Barney and I will keep to my decision. It is not because I did not feel I could live with all the disadvantages you have out-lined, dearest Caro. It is because *he* does not feel that he loves me enough to do so. So I shall take my fortune and move away from the gossips and live on my own and never marry!'

It was said defiantly, but there was an ache in her heart. In the first place she loved Hewly and the Abbey villages, and hated the thought of living away. Secondly, she loved Barney even more, but if he could not see a way clear to marrying her for love, she would not compromise. It was a bleak future but it was at least an independent one.

Caroline was looking thoughtful. 'I understand your principles, Lavender, but there is a problem. You are but three and twenty and do not come into your fortune for another two years. What is to happen in the meantime? Are you to stay here and suffer the scandal-mongering? And wherever you go, your reputation will be in shreds—'

Lavender tried to shrug it off. 'It is of no consequence. I cannot care for the petty attitudes of small-minded people…'

As if in response to her comment, the door opened and Julia Chessford entered. She smiled limpidly at Lavender.

'Good evening, Cos! Are you well? And am I to wish you happy? Judging from all the gossip, I would hope so!'

Lavender gritted her teeth. 'No, you are not, Julia! It is all a big misunderstanding…'

'Really…' Julia breathed. She plumped herself down on the opposite side of the bed to Caroline. 'Lud, how unfortunate! If you could hear what they are saying in the village—'

'Thank you, Julia,' Caroline interposed crisply. 'We have no need of your gossip. No doubt the whole will blow over shortly.'

Julia smoothed her skirts. 'I wish I had your confidence, Caro. I think Lavender is very sensible to hide herself away! You know what the villages can be like—petty, small-minded, but with long memories!'

'I know precisely,' Caroline said, looking at her pointedly, 'as I am sure you do too, Julia!'

'Still,' Julia continued, with a blithe smile at Lavender, 'I confess it is a relief to know that there will not be such a low connection in the family! For all that Barney Hammond is a prodigiously good-looking young man, he and his fortune reek of the shop! It is preferable to climb the social scale rather than slide down it!' She gave Lavender a little, cat-like smile. 'Though I do not suppose you understand the niceties of such things, cousin Lavender!'

'Was not your own father in trade, Julia?' Lavender asked crossly.

Julia waved one white hand, not a whit discomposed. 'Lud, yes! But that is precisely what I mean! I married a gentleman, and soon...' she leant forward, eyes gleaming '...I shall attach a lord!'

Lavender sighed, glad in part that the conversation had moved on from her own romantic tribulations. One could always rely on Julia to talk about herself. She found it far more interesting a subject than talking of anyone else.

'I collect that you mean to marry Lord Leverstoke,' Caroline said calmly. 'Are you so certain of him, then, Julia? And had you forgotten that Leverstoke still has a wife?'

Julia shrugged uncomfortably. 'Poor Lavinia Leverstoke is very ill, you know, and not long for this world! And everyone knows that Charles has nursed her devotedly! I am sure that no one would grudge him some happiness when she is gone...'

'So that is why you are here!' Caroline said cheerfully, winking at Lavender. 'We had all wondered why you were hiding yourself away! How discreet of you, Julia! Whilst Lady Leverstoke is dying—'

Even Julia had the grace to blush. 'You are too unkind, Caro! Why should I not have some happiness—'

'I imagine those petty and small-minded people you referred to a moment ago might have something to say about the way in which you pursue your happiness,' Caroline said, getting up and smoothing down Lavender's counterpane with an irritable hand. 'How long will dinner be, I wonder? Come, Julia, let us leave Lavender in peace! She has had a trying day and I am sure would appreciate some quiet!'

Julia was impervious to hints. She turned her huge blue eyes back on Lavender.

'Did you know, dearest Lavender, that Arthur Hammond is not really Barnabas's father? That was a polite fiction put about to save his sister's name, though I often wondered why they bothered, since the silly creature died a week after the birth!' Julia wrinkled up her nose. 'Eliza Hammond was in service somewhere over Northampton way—it could even have been Riding Park now I think of it—and came back in disgrace! Nanny Pryor knows all the tales!'

Lavender gritted her teeth. 'I have heard the gossip, Julia. It really is irrelevant—'

Julia ignored her. Her eyes lit up and she gave a little shriek. She had clearly just had a scurrilous thought. 'Oh, how piquant! I do believe it *was* Riding Park! How if the father of Eliza's child was Lord Freddie Covingham himself, and when the Covinghams showed favour to Barney recently it was on account of the irregular connection!'

'What a deal of nonsense you do talk, Julia,' Caroline said disgustedly, resting one hand on the bedpost. 'In the first place I believe that Lord Freddie and Lady Anne were but recently married at the time twenty-five years ago—'

Julia opened her eyes very wide. 'Lud, Caro, I know that you have led a sheltered life, but even you must know that there is nothing to stop a man newly-wed fathering a child on the maid!'

'I pity you your cynicism!' Caroline snapped.

Lavender wished they would cease their brangling, and if they did have to quarrel that they might do so outside her bedroom. Julia was enough to try the patience of a saint and Caroline, who was normally so placid, seemed surprisingly quick to react. Lavender went over to her. She could see tears in Caroline's hazel eyes and realised suddenly how much of a trial it must be for her sister-in-law at five months pregnant having to tolerate Julia, who was forever planting her spiteful barbs.

'Come, Caro, you must be tired,' she said gently. 'I shall go down to the kitchens and arrange for you to have dinner in your room. You must not exhaust yourself before the Covinghams get here!'

Caroline gave her a grateful look. 'Thank you, Lavender. I confess I do feel a little low in spirits.' She took the hand Lavender proffered to help her to the door. 'Oof! That's better! I declare I am growing apace—in all directions!'

Julia looked as though she was about to make some malicious observation on this, but Lavender glared pointedly at her.

'Cousin Julia, do you wish to take your supper here? Though it is my room, I am happy to lend it to you!'

Even Julia got the message this time. She got up. 'Very well! I can see I am not wanted! I shall leave the two of you together and hunt up Lewis! It will be so delightful to talk to him of old times—just the pair of us!'

'Silly piece!' Lavender said stringently as she gave Caroline her arm along the landing to the bedroom. 'Lewis will not thank her for inflicting her company on him! How much longer must she stay, Caro? Can we not find a way to persuade her to go?'

'I shall spend my evening thinking on it!' Caroline agreed, sinking down into a fireside chair with a sigh of relief. 'She must be made to go or we shall all run mad!' She patted Lavender's hand. 'I have not forgot, my love, that you are the one who has a dilemma to deal with now! If you wish to speak to me—' She broke off, a twinkle in her eye. 'Oh dear, does that stubborn look mean that you have made up your mind? The times I have seen Lewis look just the same…'

Lavender laughed. 'I fear so, Caro. I am still of the same mind. I shall not marry Mr Hammond.'

Caroline shrugged. 'So be it. We shall see what comes. I hope that Julia's ill-bred remarks about his parentage did not offend you?'

Lavender shook her head. 'To tell the truth, I ought to thank her for it!' She saw Caroline's look of surprise and smiled. 'She reminded me of the book you see— With all the other events, I had quite forgot to ask Mr Hammond where he had obtained it from! Yet if it were amongst his mother's effects and she had been in service, she might well have taken it from Kenton Hall—'

'Julia said that she was in service at Riding Park, not at Kenton,' Caroline said slowly. She looked up at Lavender. 'Still, it is a good thought! We shall ask Lady Anne when she comes, for I do not for a minute believe Julia's scandalous assertion that Barney Hammond is Lord Freddie's son!'

'I should think not!' Lavender made her way to the door. 'The Covinghams are far too unfashionably fond of each other for such a tale to ring true!'

'Besides,' Caroline said with a smile, 'Barney does not have the Covingham nose! One might as well suggest that he was Sir Thomas Kenton's by-blow!' Her smile faded. 'Now there is a thought…'

Lavender was laughing to think of the unworldly

baronet siring an illegitimate son. 'How your mind does run on, Caro! I fear that if Barney is the natural child of any nobleman, the Marquis of Sywell must still be the prime candidate!' She sighed. 'Do you have any rose water that I might borrow? I fear that Julia has left me with the most dreadful headache!'

'I had hoped to find you in better spirits, my dearest Lavender,' Frances Covingham said plaintively, holding her friend at arm's length and eyeing her closely. 'You look as wan as December! Now, what is all this gossip I hear about you? To think I always found the country slow!'

Frances slipped her hand through Lavender's arm and steered her away up the stairs. 'Take me to your room so that we can have a coze together! I hear that Mrs Chessford is staying with you? What bad luck!'

It was the following day and the Covinghams had arrived a half hour previously for a stay of a few days. It seemed that the atmosphere in the house had lightened immediately. Caroline was delighted to see Anne again and Lewis had immediately taken Lord Freddie off to have a look at the estate.

'We shall soon have you in plump currant again,' Frances continued as they reached the top of the stairs and went along the landing. 'Lady Perceval, whom we called upon on our way here, said that she never listens to village gossip and that you were not to regard it. But *before* we disregard it, dearest Lavender, I want to hear all about it!'

Lavender laughed despite herself. 'It is not a matter for funning, you know, Frances!' she said wryly. 'I am not at all sure that your mama should let you associate with me, for I am in the most horrible disgrace!'

'Stuff!' Frances said staunchly. 'Mama is not such a high stickler to cut up rough about such silly rumours! She was more concerned to be trapped under the same roof as your cousin!'

Lavender smothered a giggle. There was something about Frances that was very reviving to her spirits. The younger girl was irrepressibly cheerful, and now her curious gaze was taking in Lavender's bedroom and she was nodding appreciatively.

'Oh, what a charming room! You are so fortunate, Lavender! And the view! I declare it is as fine as any in Northamptonshire!' She spun round and settled at the foot of the bed where Caroline had sat the night before, leaning her arms against the wooden rest. Lavender sat down opposite.

'So tell me what has been happening,' Frances wheedled. 'I hear it involves that delightful Mr Hammond! Do you think you might marry him, Lavender? Oh, lucky you—'

'Frances!' Lavender said, trying to sound strict but failing utterly. She smiled. 'I tell you, this is no matter for amusement—'

'I know! I am a hoyden!' Frances leant her chin on her hand. 'But truly I thought him such a very charming gentleman!' She shivered pleasurably. 'It seems to me that most gentlemen are all surface and no substance, but with Mr Hammond it is deeper than that! In fact I would have quite a *tendre* for him myself, and no doubt would bore you rigid with the repetition of his name were it not that I am still hopelessly in love with Mr Oliver!'

'Have you seen Mr Oliver since the night of the ball?' Lavender enquired.

Frances's face fell. 'No indeed, for Mama has been odiously strict, you know! He did call, but she would not allow me to see him so I was not able to tell him that we would be in London from next week and he should contrive to meet me there—'

'Oh, Frances!'

'Well…' Miss Covingham looked defensive '…I must see him again, Lavender, positively I must! In fact I am hoping that as he is such a good friend of your Mr Hammond, he might be in this very neighbourhood! Who knows! But—' she frowned '—I know you are trying to distract me! Now tell me the whole story!'

Lavender told her, not the whole story, but most of it, and Frances nodded and prompted and made sympathetic noises. At the end of it she said with a sigh, 'I can see that you feel you must refuse him, Lavender dearest, but now you are prey to these wretched gossips! You should face them out, you know!' Her eyes brightened. 'Oh, the very thing! The Percevals sent a card with us, you know, inviting us all to dinner—'

'Oh no!' Lavender knew she looked horrified. Ever since the gossip had broken, she had been possessed of a cowardly fear to step outside the house. She had certainly no intention of going into Abbot Quincey, or even going out into company. Yet if she was going to stay at Hewly until she came into her fortune she would have to go outside at some point. She could hardly skulk about the house for another two years.

'Well—' Frances put her head on one side '—perhaps we could start with a walk! I have no intention of allowing any friend of mine to become a recluse!'

She picked up the botany book, which Lavender had been keeping on her bedside table. 'Is this the book you mentioned just now, Lavender? The keepsake from Mr Hammond?' She bent her head over it, chestnut curls brushing the pages. 'It is so romantic of him…'

'The book has a mysterious history, if not a romantic one,' Lavender commented, smiling, 'and one that may involve Riding Park!' She told Frances briefly of their visit from Sir Thomas Kenton and of Julia's reminisces about Eliza.

'Of course, it is all very tenuous,' she said at the

end. 'Though Mr Hammond had the book from his mother, I have no idea how she came by it! For it was certainly Sir Thomas's book originally—' She broke off, shaking her head.

'Perhaps Mr Hammond has inherited other things from his mother!' Frances interposed, eyes huge with excitement. 'Maybe he has a whole chest of her effects locked away—books, clothes, a lock of her hair…'

'How Gothic!' Lavender tried not to laugh. Frances looked offended.

'Pray do not make fun of me, I am trying to solve the mystery!'

'I do not wish to discourage you,' Lavender said, 'but it is unlikely that Eliza Hammond would have been able to read a book of botany written in Latin!'

Frances looked cross. 'She might have borrowed it—'

'You mean stolen it—from her employer's library?'

'I mean borrowed…or had it given to her by someone!' Frances wriggled with excitement. 'Yes, I have it! The book was given to her by her lover!'

Lavender frowned. 'Then that would have been Sir Thomas Kenton, and that is foolish—'

'Why so? Was Sir Thomas above a dalliance with a maid?'

'Frances—'

'I wonder if Mama and Papa have any connections

with the Kentons,' Frances swept on. 'Perhaps they will remember Eliza Hammond. If she had been in service at Riding Park it would have been just after they were married, I suppose. Lord, what a sad tale. The poor girl, pregnant and abandoned by her lover, then dying so soon after giving birth!' The ready tears stood out in her eyes. 'And poor Mr Hammond, forever deprived of the knowledge of his father's identity!'

'I daresay that sometimes it is better not to know.' Lavender got up and moved over to the window. A dark cloud was edging across the sun.

'Oh but surely… A foundling is never sure of his place in the world…' Frances, with all the wealth and position of the Covingham family behind her, could only pity someone with no such certain place.

'Then one must carve a place for oneself, I suppose.' Lavender watched as the sky darkened and the rain started to fall. That was what Barney had been trying to do, she knew, with his studies and his ambitions to be a pharmacist. It was admirable and she knew that many a lesser man would have crumbled sooner, accepted his place on Hammond's charity and not sought more. She sighed. Her money would have enabled Barney to achieve his ambitions so much more quickly, allowing him to achieve his profession and support a wife. If only he would have taken that chance! They could have moved away— away from Abbot Quincey with its gossiping tongues that would never let them forget the forced and foolish match. She knew they could have been happy.

She sighed again. 'This is just idle speculation, and confusing at that! It gets us nowhere—'

'Then we must ask Mr Hammond!' Frances jumped up. 'Let us go at once! I shall fetch my bonnet—'

'It is raining,' Lavender said, watching with some relief as the drops tumbled from the dark sky. 'Perhaps later. Frances—' she put out a hand to the younger girl '—pray do not tell anyone of this! I do not like to gossip about Mr Hammond and we have only been imagining—'

Frances looked offended. 'Tell anyone? Why, Lavender, as though I would! You know I am the soul of discretion! I swear I shall not say a word!'

Chapter Nine

'Mama,' Frances said later that evening, sitting beside her mother on the sofa in the drawing-room, 'do you remember a housemaid by the name of Eliza Hammond? She would have been at Riding Park…oh, some six and twenty years ago!'

Lavender, who had been sitting across from her, discussing painting with Lord Freddie, looked up sharply. She should have known that Frances's ideas of discretion and her own were vastly different. Frances returned her suspicious look with one of bland innocence.

'Eliza Hammond?' Lady Anne said vaguely. 'I do not believe so, my love, but then I have so tiresomely poor a memory! And maids do come and go, you know… Why do you ask?'

Lavender started to speak at random, but Frances ploughed on doggedly. 'It is just that it seems she was our Mr Hammond's mother and was once in service with you. Oh, Mama—' she fixed Lady Anne with a pleading glance '—it is particularly important that you remember—'

Lady Anne frowned, pushing her *pince nez* further up her nose. 'Hmm. Twenty-six years, you say? I would have been a new bride then!' She smiled fondly. 'Wait… There was a girl—dark, very lady-like, quiet-spoken… Would that have been Matilda?'

'Eliza!' Frances corrected. 'Really, Mama!'

'Yes—' Lady Anne ignored her '—I recall her now, because she was so genteel that the Duchess— your grandmother, Frances—used to comment that people would think her better bred than her employers! And she probably was, for the Covinghams were all rogues a few generations back, and—'

'Yes, Mama,' Frances pleaded, 'but Eliza Hammond?'

'She left to get married shortly after I went to Riding Park,' Lady Anne said placidly. 'Is that what you wished to know, my love?'

Lavender and Frances exchanged a look. 'Left to get married, ma'am?' Lavender queried. 'Are you certain that she was not—' She broke off, blushing.

'What Lavender means, Mama,' Frances said impatiently, 'is that we thought Eliza Hammond had been turned off because she was *enceinte!* Are you certain this is the same girl?'

Their discussion was now drawing attention. Lavender saw Julia, who had been discussing mutual friends with Caroline, tilt her head in their direction, scenting gossip like a fox scenting prey. Lady Anne leaned forward to address her husband.

'Freddie, do you recall—'

'Eliza Hammond?' Lord Freddie nodded. 'Not that I am in the way of remembering such things, but I do remember her! Because of the scandal, my dear! Do you not recollect?'

This time Lavender saw Julia smile with satisfied malice. She felt increasingly desperate. It seemed quite improper to be discussing Barney Hammond's mother with such freedom in public. The poor woman could scarce defend her reputation and Barney himself would no doubt have been furious and mortified to think her the centre of such attention. Lavender was about to beg a change of subject when something Lord Freddie was saying caught her attention.

'…Left the Park to marry John Kenton,' he said cheerfully. 'Of course, we all thought him a fool, for his family were as poor as sparrows and his father most particularly insisted on him marrying a fortune, and what should the poor fool do but fall in love with a maid! Still, there was no arguing with him and the last I heard of it he was travelling home to get his father's blessing on the proposed match!'

There was a silence followed by chatter as everyone talked at once.

'Of course! I remember the whole now!' Lady Anne said triumphantly.

'Married the maid? How piquant!' This was Julia, looking torn between excitement and disappointment that Eliza Hammond appeared to have been respectably married after all.

'John Kenton? But surely that must be Sir Thomas's son…' Lavender was saying hesitantly to Caroline, whilst Frances said jubilantly, 'Then that is how she came by the book!'

Lewis raised his voice sharply to demand quiet. Everyone looked at him expectantly.

'My apologies,' Lewis said easily, smiling at their startled faces, 'if my appeal sounds more at home on a quarterdeck than in a drawing-room! I feel, however, that this may be rather important! Lord Freddie, can you tell us a little about John Kenton himself?'

Lord Freddie looked mildly surprised. 'Why, of course, old chap! Kenton was a bookish fellow who was forever off on mad trips about the world. Lord, it must be a matter of twenty-five years since he died! Disappeared in the South Americas somewhere, I heard, and his servants swore he was eaten!' He shook his head. 'Pity! He was a good fellow!'

'But what became of his wife?' Caroline asked. 'If he had married Eliza Hammond, where was she whilst he was abroad? And if John was the son of our Sir Thomas Kenton, why does Sir Thomas know nothing of his grandson?'

Lavender's shoulders slumped. 'Perhaps is just a coincidence and there is no family connection, Caro?'

'Perhaps so.' Caroline looked round the assembled group. 'Before we speculate further can I pour more tea for anyone? I find it helps the mental processes marvellously!'

'Sir Thomas mentioned that his sons had both died,' Lewis put in, when all the cups had been replenished. 'Perhaps one of them was John Kenton—'

'He was!' Lavender said suddenly. 'Do you not remember, Lewis? Sir Thomas said that he had lent the botanical volume to his son John—'

'Could be another family, all the same,' Lewis opined. 'John is a common enough name.'

'Was he a friend of yours, Lord Frederick?' Lavender asked carefully.

Lord Freddie nodded. 'One of my closest friends at Oxford, Miss Brabant! He was a bookish fellow, much cleverer than I! He always had an interest in odd fauna and flora, particularly the flora! That was why he was forever travelling, to collect specimens. On one trip he discovered that the bark of a particular tree was most efficacious against pain. Poor fellow!' He laughed. 'He was so excited and we were all so uninterested! And his parents!' Lord Freddie's laughter faded away. 'His father threatened to cut him off without a penny if he did not stay at home and act the gentleman, and his mother worried herself into her grave over him, for she knew he would come to a bad end!'

'Where was his home, Papa?' Frances asked, sitting forward and fixing him with a look. 'That would surely help us tell whether the family is the same one—'

'Kenton? Why just down the road, I believe!' Lord Freddie scratched his head. 'Is not the village of that name some ten miles distant? I know the Kentons held the Manor there since the Domesday, but whether they are still there... As I say, John was the younger son, and his mother died when I still knew him. What became of his father and brother, I cannot say.'

Lavender's heart was beating very fast. 'Oh surely—this must be the same family! There are too many coincidences otherwise! But I do not understand...' She frowned. How had Eliza Hammond, who had apparently left Riding Park to marry, ended up pregnant and alone, throwing herself on her brother's mercy?

'Why all the interest, my love?' Lord Freddie was asking his daughter. 'I had not thought of John Kenton for nigh on twenty years!'

Frances indicated Lavender's botany book.

'It is just that Miss Brabant has been given this book,' Frances said, gesturing towards it, 'and wondered to whom it had originally belonged. It has the Kenton coat of arms at the front, you see, and was originally in the possession of Mr Hammond. Apparently he had inherited it from his mother.'

'Botany, eh?' Lord Freddie was flicking through the pages. 'Yes, this would be John's book, all right and tight. Just his sort of thing! And you say it was given to Mr Hammond by his mother?' He looked at Lavender. 'That is very suggestive, is it not, Miss Brabant?'

Lavender's throat was suddenly dry. It was indeed suggestive that Eliza had married John Kenton and had had the book of botany from him, handing it on to her own child, Sir Thomas's grandson.

'But I do not understand!' she burst out. 'If Miss Hammond and Mr Kenton were married then why was she obliged to return to her brother's house for the birth of her child? And why did she never tell anyone of the wedding—'

She broke off in confusion at the looks of sympathy on the faces of the others, all except for Julia who looked maliciously speculative. Caroline put her teacup down gently. 'I think we must consider, dearest Lavender, the possibility that the wedding did not take place. Lord Freddie has indicated that Sir Thomas wanted his son to marry a fortune. How if John Kenton had failed to gain his father's permission to the match and regretted his plan to marry Eliza—'

'And abandoned her, pregnant and penniless!'

Julia finished, clapping her hands. 'Oh yes, I like that idea!'

Everyone looked at her with unconcealed dislike.

'It does seem the most likely solution,' Frances said despondently. 'Poor Eliza! And poor Mr Hammond! It is not fair!'

Caroline fixed Lavender with a kindly look. 'I do feel that it would be best to speak to Mr Hammond about this, Lavender! Possibly Sir Thomas might hold the answer, but I do not feel that you should approach him behind Mr Hammond's back!' She took a sip of tea. 'When Sir Thomas first laid claim to the book I thought it most odd, and now we appear to have filled in the whole background to the tale without the slightest notion of whether or not we are in the right of it! Ten to one there is another explanation that Mr Hammond will furnish if only he is asked!'

'There is a picture of John Kenton at Riding Park,' Lord Freddie said suddenly. 'In the gallery, by the one of you as a girl, my love…' He smiled at Lady Anne. 'It is only small, but a good likeness—'

'Of course!' Lavender exclaimed. 'I was looking at it on the night of the ball! A dark gentleman with striking features—'

'Did he look like Mr Hammond?' Frances asked eagerly.

Lavender shook her head, smiling. 'I cannot really be sure. Nanny Pryor, my old nurse, says that Mr

Hammond's looks come from his mother's side of the family…'

Frances looked cast down.

'All the more reason,' Caroline said briskly, 'to speak to Mr Hammond about the book as soon as you can, Lavender. I am sure this mystery can be solved without any further speculation on our part!'

The conversation became general once more, but Lavender sat quietly drinking her tea and did not join in. The prospect of seeing Barney again was daunting enough, without trying to explain to him how she came to be expressing such a curious interest in his family history. Judging by his pride on previous occasions, she was sure it was not an interest that he would welcome. It would be much easier to approach Sir Thomas Kenton and ask him to provide the information on John's history, but she knew Caroline was right. Barney had to be made aware of the situation first and Lavender's heart sank at the thought of it.

Despite all Lavender's prayers for rain, the following morning was dry. Frances was adamant that they were to walk into Abbot Quincey and quiz Barney Hammond on the origin of his book, and although Lavender hung back from the proposed trip, she thought it only fair to acquaint him with his possible connection with the Kenton family.

It was a lovely day. The sun was bright and warm

and the hedgerows were full of birds, but for once Lavender did not wish to stop and enjoy the sights and sounds of the country. The roads were a little muddy, and after a mile Frances was already complaining that it was an unconscionable distance. To Lavender it seemed all too short. In no time they were in Abbot Quincey and walking up the main street, and she was glad of the moral support of Frances and Lady Anne.

'Back straight, chin up!' She could imagine the Admiral admonishing her as she walked past the curious stares of the passers-by. 'Nothing to be ashamed of, girl!'

Lavender straightened her back and looked directly ahead of her, yet even as she was walking past the Angel inn and the bakers and the milliners she was wondering which of these people had seen her with Barney at the pool and had hurried to spread their gossip.

The draper's shop was busy and it seemed that all conversation ceased as they crossed the threshold. Lavender's gaze had gone immediately to the counter, where Arthur Hammond was serving a customer. Of Barney himself there was no sign. Lavender did not know whether to be glad or sorry, and part of her simply wanted to turn and run.

Arthur Hammond looked up and his florid face registered indecision. It was the first occasion on which Lavender had ever seen him display hesitation when confronted by customers from the nobility. Clearly her own position was now equivocal since she had refused to marry his adoptive son, and no doubt he was still smarting over the way that Lewis had summarily evicted him from Hewly. On the other hand, Lady Anne and Miss Covingham were too important to be ignored. He hovered, came forward, fell back again, and finally brought himself to address them.

'Ladies,' he pointedly refused to look directly at Lavender, 'how may I help you?'

Lady Anne and Frances both looked at Lavender, who was hoping that she might quietly sink through the floor.

'I would like… I had hoped…to see Mr Barnabas Hammond…'

A whisper ran through the other customers, who had edged closer to listen, pretending an interest in the bolts of material that were closest to where Lavender stood. Arthur Hammond's face hardened with dislike.

'My son is from home! Beg pardon, Miss Brabant, but I have work to attend to and no time for idle chatter!'

Lady Anne looked down her nose at him and swept the two girls out of the shop without further ado.

'That man is so unpleasantly pushing and rag-mannered,' she observed crossly. 'Remind me not to patronise his shops again, Frances!'

'Yes, Mama.' Frances seemed quite cast down for once. 'You might at least have made a push to discover where Mr Hammond had gone, Lavender!' she whispered under her breath. 'Now we shall never solve the mystery!'

Lavender did not reply. She was feeling so miserable that she would happily have left the mystery of Barney's parentage where it belonged—in the past. First she had bolstered herself up to see him, then her hopes had been dashed by Hammond, and the whole experience had been so unpleasant that she thought she would never set foot in the draper's shop again. It was fortunate that she had already bought herself so many hats and gloves—now she need not go shopping for several years.

'I am to call on Lady Perceval,' Lady Anne said as they reached the gates of the Hall. 'Do you girls wish to accompany me?'

'No, thank you, Mama,' Frances said listlessly, after a glance at Lavender's face. 'We shall go back to Hewly.'

'Very well. Make sure that you return directly and do not wander—'

'No, Mama…'

'And do not take a short cut through the woods and become lost—'

'No, Mama…'

'And I shall see you shortly. No doubt I shall take the carriage back…'

'Yes, Mama…'

They walked on in silence and Lavender was glad that Frances had the delicacy not to chatter. For once her irrepressible friend seemed as cast down as she.

It was the sound of hooves upon the road that drew them both from their respective apathy. Frances caught Lavender's arm and pulled her on to the grass verge and almost into the hedge.

'Lavender, be careful!' Her voice lifted. 'Well, upon my word! It is Mr Hammond—and Mr Oliver!'

Lavender had never seen Barney riding before and had not even known he could. The thought brought a slight smile to her lips, for was it not just another of his secrets? He sat the black hunter with ease and competence, and beside him James Oliver brought his grey under control with a slight touch on the rein. He raised his hat.

'Miss Covingham! Miss Brabant! This is the most delightful surprise!'

Casting a fleeting glance at Barney's face, Lavender felt that his surprise was not of the delightful sort. His dark gaze was resting on her, but with none of the warmth or pleasure that she would have hoped to see. This was decidedly awkward. She had wondered what her reception would be and now she knew. He had reluctantly proposed and she had refused and now there was nothing left but cold pride.

James Oliver dismounted with alacrity, to loop his reins over his arm and walk alongside Frances with a touchingly eager pleasure. Barney on the other hand looked as though he might ride straight past with only the slightest of acknowledgements. Then, evidently succumbing to his own innate courtesy, he swung down from the saddle and came to stand beside her.

'Miss Brabant. You are well?'

'Yes, I thank you, sir…' Lavender could feel the colour coming into her face, the embarrassment that made it almost impossible to look at him. She made an effort. 'And you? I hope… That is… I hope you are well also?'

'Yes, thank you.'

There was a silence, in marked contrast to the chatter of Frances and Mr Oliver, who were strolling ahead. It was evidently Mr Oliver's intention to walk with them back to Hewly, and suddenly it seemed to Lavender a very long way to be filled with silences. She was going to have to broach the matter of the book, if only to pass the time. She cleared her throat.

'Mr Hammond, it is timely that we should meet, for there was something that I wished to ask you.'

'Yes, Miss Brabant?'

Lavender thought that Barney sounded ever-so-slightly bored.

'It is about the book that you gave me. I wondered about it because I remember you telling me that you inherited it from your mother, yet it has the arms of Kenton inside the cover. Do you know anything more of its history?'

Barney looked blank. Worse, Lavender thought, he looked totally uninterested. 'I fear not, Miss Brabant.'

Lavender sighed. It was going to be even more difficult than she had anticipated if he was going to answer her in monosyllables.

'Are you certain? It could be very important! You see—' She took a deep breath. 'Sir Thomas Kenton saw the book when he called at Hewly, and claimed that it had once been in his library. He had given it to his son John. Yet the book was left to you by your mother and there must be some mystery here—'

'I do not imagine so.' Barney glanced down at her, his dark eyes indifferent. 'No doubt this John Kenton left the book somewhere and my mother picked it up from curiosity—or perhaps tidiness! She was a housemaid, after all!' Now Lavender heard some feeling in his voice, the anger of a man who was tired of being reminded of the scandal and mystery of his birth. No doubt Arthur Hammond had never ceased to remind him of his mother's disgrace and his own charity. She hesitated, on the verge of giving up, but something made her persist.

'I am sorry if my interest seems ill-bred—'

'It does!' Barney sounded plainly angry now. 'In

fact, Miss Brabant, it seems damnably impertinent! Can you not just leave well alone?'

He had not raised his voice, but the hard edge to it made Lavender's eyes smart. She had already been upset by Arthur Hammond's rudeness and now Barney's contempt and lack of interest caught her on the raw.

'There is no cause for such discourtesy! I am only trying to help you, for it seems that John Kenton may have been your father!'

Barney dropped the horse's reins and spun round on her. He caught her wrist in a grip that felt bruising.

'And how will being the bastard son of this John Kenton help me, Miss Brabant? Do you know how many times I have tortured myself with thoughts of my father—doubt, speculation enough to drive a man to madness? How many times do you think that my uncle has spoken of my mother's shame and the fact that she did not—could not—name her lover? I am sick with the thought of it all!' His furious gaze pinned Lavender to the spot. 'Do you think that knowing the name of the man who dishonoured her would make me one whit more acceptable as the suitor of an Admiral's daughter? I think not! So cease your investigations, I beg, and do not pry into my history!'

Lavender stared at him. Wrapped up in her own unhappiness, it had not occurred to her that Barney might still be feeling bitter that he had nothing to offer her. She had thought herself so much better and braver than he for being prepared to dare all for his love. Now she saw that his torment sprung from the fact that he loved her just as much as she loved him but he would not relent until he felt he had something better to give her. The problem of his parentage just seemed to make matters more intractable. She put a hand on his arm.

'Barney, you know that I—'

'No!' He shook her off furiously. 'Lavender, I mean what I say! Do not interfere! And do not speak to me about this again!'

'He seemed very angry,' Frances said, awed, as they strolled in the Hewly Manor gardens that afternoon. 'To think I had imagined Mr Hammond as the most placid gentleman in the world!' She gave a giggle. 'When he mounted his horse and took off across country like that I wondered what could possibly have happened! And all James could do was lament that the horse was one of the best in his stables, and like as not it would break a leg!'

Lavender gave a wan smile. 'Well, I suppose I am well served for prying into Mr Hammond's business! What man would care to have his antecedents picked over in such a way? I knew it yet still I persisted! It will be best to leave well alone now!'

Frances looked horrified. 'Oh, no, you cannot do

that! Why, ten to one we shall find that Eliza and John Kenton were married and that Mr Hammond is heir to a fortune! Oh, Lavender, do not give up now!'

Lavender shook her head. She pushed open the gate into the lavender walk and the two girls strolled up the stone path to the house. The heads of lavender were dead and grey, their scent faint now in the autumn. Lavender tried to lift her spirits.

'You seemed to be getting on marvellously well with Mr Oliver, Frances—until your mama came along in the Perceval carriage!'

Frances smiled mischievously. 'Yes, was that not bad luck! Mama looked quite put out! Still, I had the chance to tell Mr Oliver of our address in London, and he assures me he will contrive a meeting during the Little Season!' She frowned a little. 'I think him quite sincere, you know, and for all Mama's concerns I am no silly miss to throw my bonnet over a windmill!'

Lavender thought that she was probably right. Frances was bright and insouciant but she was no fool, and no doubt Lady Anne would come round to the merits of the match. James Oliver might not have a title but he was as well connected as the Covinghams themselves and had a very tidy estate in Hertfordshire.

'Now, Lavender,' Frances was saying briskly, 'there is only one more day before we leave for London and I must, positively must, get to the bottom of the Kenton mystery! So I have decided that there is only one thing for it!'

Lavender felt her heart sinking. Frances was a dear girl and a great friend, but she was also totally incorrigible.

'Sir Thomas Kenton must hold the key to all this!' Frances was saying. 'And as he has already invited you to call, dearest Lavender, we may take him up on his offer tomorrow! It is decided! We are going to Kenton!'

Chapter Ten

Not surprisingly, Frances's plan to visit Kenton the
following day was greeted with disapproval. She was
already in her mother's bad books for having been
found in conversation with Mr Oliver, and Lady
Anne expressed the strong conviction that Frances
should cease to behave like a hoyden and spend the
day quietly resting before their journey.

During the late morning, whilst the ladies were
taking a gentle stroll in the gardens, Frances grabbed
Lavender's arm and pulled her through the doorway
into one of the walled orchards.

'Lavender, I am resolved that we should go to
Kenton in spite of everything!' she whispered. 'It is
the only way! If we visit Sir Thomas he may be able
to throw some light on the matter!'

'Your mama—' Lavender began.

'Oh fie! We need not tell her!' Frances's eyes were
bright. 'Mrs Brabant always rests in the afternoons

and like as not the other ladies will retire to their rooms! Mama certainly will if Mrs Chessford is about! I heard the gentlemen say that they plan to go out riding so they will not be back before dinner… It is ideal! We may ride over to Kenton in an hour and be back before nightfall!'

Lavender swallowed hard. 'I do not believe I have quite your spirit of adventure, dear Frances! But I am happy to take the carriage!'

Frances looked disappointed. Clearly a staid carriage drive did not fit with her ideas of romantic adventure.

'Oh, very well! I suppose that is better than nothing! Be sure to be ready directly after luncheon—pretend that you are taking a rest, then creep out to join me in the stable yard!'

That the plan worked at all was largely due to the fact that Caroline's rooms faced west, away from the courtyard, and that she and Lady Anne were enjoying a chat in privacy. Julia, meanwhile, had driven into Abbot Quincey on an errand and the gentlemen were away across the other side of the estate. Lavender was tolerably certain that no one had seen them go.

'Mama will be up on her high ropes when she finds out!' Frances said gleefully, as the countryside rolled past. 'But by then we may have solved the mystery of Mr Hammond's ancestry! Oh, Lavender, it is so exciting!'

Lavender was not so sure. She was aware that she

was behaving in an irresponsible manner ill-suited to a lady of three and twenty, and that she could be considered to be leading Miss Covingham astray. The fact that it had been Frances's idea to take the secret journey to Kenton was beside the point, for she could hardly blame her friend when the recriminations started. She clenched her hands on her reticule. Then there was the fact that she was going against Barney's expressed wishes, and that they might come away with no more idea of what had happened than they had had before... Lavender sat on the edge of her seat and wished for a more resilient spirit.

It was only ten miles to Kenton, and Lavender was still having serious misgivings by the time that the carriage drove through the trim village around the green, past the small stone church, and in at the gates of Kenton Hall. The stone wall was tumbledown and the deer park beyond was a mass of grass and wild flowers. Evidently Sir Thomas had neglected his grounds for his books, for the whole estate had about it an air of charming neglect.

The house came into view at the end of the drive, a compact building with golden stone and a red roof, much of it covered in ivy. The carriage sweep was thick with weeds. The girls got out and stood on the gravel. The first thing that struck Lavender was that it was quite silent; the house was shuttered and there was no sound but for the harsh cry of a peacock from the gardens.

Frances, whose yearning for adventure seemed suddenly to have deserted her, was looking about her a little apprehensively.

'Perhaps Sir Thomas is from home? Lavender, shall we go back, now, at once—'

'We cannot turn round and go tamely home now!' Lavender walked up to the oak front door and reached out decisively to pull the bell. She heard it jangle away in the depths of the house but there was no response. Sir Thomas, it seemed, was not at home.

'Oh, there is someone down in the gardens!' Frances was clutching her arm rather in the manner of someone about to run away. 'Perhaps… Do you think…'

'It is Sir Thomas!' Lavender caught sight of the figure of Sir Thomas Kenton as he crossed the terrace and strolled down a grassy walk towards the lake. He was carrying a book, his head was bent, and he had evidently not noticed his visitors at all.

'Sir Thomas!' Lavender turned away from the door and hurried across the drive to the small path that led through a gateway into the formal gardens. Around this, the east wing of the house, the gardens were more neatly kept, with box hedges and clipped lawns. Now that she was closer, Lavender could hear Sir Thomas reading aloud in Latin as he walked. He looked a little startled to be accosted from a great distance, but then his face broke into a broad smile.

'Miss Brabant! What a delightful surprise, my dear! How do you do?'

'Sir Thomas—' Lavender hurried forward to shake his hand. 'How are you, sir?' She drew Frances forward. 'This is Miss Covingham. Pray excuse us for arriving without warning—'

'Not at all, my dear!' Sir Thomas beamed at them. He tucked his book away under his arm. 'I am enchanted to have some company for afternoon tea! There are late strawberries from the hot houses, you know, in sore need of eating!'

He shepherded them up a straight path between tall hedges, up a wide sweep of stone steps and on to the terrace.

'Have you driven over from Hewly?' Sir Thomas asked, as he gestured for them to precede him through the long door leading into the library. 'It is a pleasant journey, is it not—at least in the sunshine!' He laughed. 'I cannot believe that I was so unlucky to have become marooned so close to home—'

'But indeed your poor luck was our good fortune, sir,' Lavender said quickly, 'and it also explains our intrusion here, for we have something very particular to ask of you!'

Sir Thomas looked intrigued. 'Then have a seat and acquaint me with it, my dear!' he said comfortably. 'But first I shall send for tea!'

He rang the bell for the maid and asked for afternoon tea and strawberries, whilst Lavender and Frances looked about them with ill-concealed curiosity. The library was a long, rectangular room with huge, high bookshelves and piles of volumes stacked up on the floor. There were windows at either end, but it was a dark room, made darker by heavy old furniture and gloomy hangings.

Sir Thomas returned his book to the top of one pile and fussed around, making sure that his unexpected guests were comfortable on the gold and gilt sofas.

'I so seldom have guests,' he murmured. 'It is about time that the house heard some voices and laughter again.'

'Oh, Lavender, look!'

Lavender had caught sight of the picture at the same time as Frances spoke. It was hanging to the right of the fireplace, a portrait of a man in the dress of the mid-eighteenth century. He was very dark, with hair so brown it was almost black, and deep brown eyes.

'Why,' Frances sounded quite amazed, 'it is the image of Mr Hammond!'

Sir Thomas looked to see what had attracted their attention.

'The portrait of Sir Barnabas Kenton? He was my father…'

'Sir Barnabas!' Frances said excitedly. 'Lavender, tell Sir Thomas the story at once!'

Sir Thomas turned his gentle blue gaze on her. 'Dear me, Miss Brabant, you both seem most perplexed by some matter. How may I help? Oh, but wait—tea first, tales later!'

The maid had returned with the tea, served in delicate china cups, and a huge bowl of strawberries and cream. Frances helped herself eagerly, but Lavender found that apprehension had blunted her appetite. She pressed her hands together to prevent their trembling.

'Now,' Sir Thomas said to Lavender, once they were all settled. 'What is this tale you have to tell, my dear? I am quite agog!'

'Well.' Lavender took a sustaining draught of tea. 'I wanted to ask about your son, Sir Thomas. Your younger son, I believe—Mr John Kenton? Was he ever married?' She saw Sir Thomas's look of blank puzzlement and hurried on. 'Forgive me, the question must seem most impertinent, and indeed it would be, but—'

Frances lost patience with Lavender's circumspection at this point. 'What Miss Brabant is trying to tell you, Sir Thomas, is that she—we—believe that your son John was married to a Miss Eliza Hammond of Abbot Quincey! We wondered if you could help us—confirm whether or not the story is true?'

Sir Thomas had turned quite pale, so pale that

Lavender put down her cup quickly and went across to his side. She felt a pang of concern, for the baronet was old and frail and Frances had sprung the news rather suddenly.

'Sir Thomas? Are you quite well, sir?'

'Good heavens, good heavens….' Sir Thomas was murmuring. 'I tried to find her, but there was no trace… And you say that she was in Abbot Quincey all the time? But how could that be, and Knottingley not know?'

Lavender put a hand on his. She was shaking with a mixture of hope and fear. 'Then is it true, sir? For there is something else you should know. Eliza had a son—'

There came the sound of a bell jangling throughout the house. Lavender and Frances exchanged a look, but Sir Thomas did not appear to even notice. He looked old and confused, and Lavender was suddenly afraid that their news had been too much for him.

'A son?' He spoke in a whisper. 'A son of John's? But how—'

The door opened. A butler, who looked as ancient and dusty as his master, stood in the doorway.

'I beg your pardon, Sir Thomas, but you have some visitors.' He sounded vaguely surprised at such an unusual circumstance. 'Lord Frederick Covingham, Lady Anne Covingham, Mr and Mrs Lewis Brabant.'

Frances's face was the picture of guilt. She put down the bowl of strawberries and stood up hastily. Lewis and Caroline were greeting Sir Thomas warmly, and Lord Freddie was shaking the baronet by the hand and explaining that he had once been a friend of John's. Lavender was glad to see that Sir Thomas was less frail than he looked, for he greeted the new arrivals with some animation and hastily ordered more tea. She was less pleased that the new arrivals had appeared before she and Frances had got to the root of the mystery, for now it seemed they might be summarily marched home, strawberries notwithstanding.

'Really, Lavender, this mad start is very unlike you!' Caroline complained once they were all settled again and the tea served. Her glance slid to Frances and she tried not to smile. 'We knew at once where you must have gone, for with Frances's insistence that you visit Kenton today, there could be no doubt! What has come over the pair of you? This escapade does credit to neither of you!'

Lavender, reflecting that Caroline must have been an authoritative governess, tried to apologise.

'I am sorry if we gave you cause for concern, Caro, but we both wished to find out about the history of John and Eliza—'

'The two of you are obsessed with this business,' Caroline commented. She smiled at Sir Thomas. 'I do hope, Sir Thomas, that the girls have not troubled you—'

Lavender grimaced at Frances. She felt about twelve and still in the schoolroom.

'Not at all, dear ma'am,' Sir Thomas was smiling gently. 'We had, however, reached a critical point in our discussions, for Miss Brabant had just asked me if my son John had ever been married, and suggested that he had a son!'

'Lavender,' Caroline said in a failing voice, 'I cannot believe you had so little delicacy—'

'I am sorry, but we cannot regard all that now, Caro!' Lavender leant forward urgently. 'Sir Thomas was about to tell us what he knew...'

Sir Thomas sighed. 'Yes, I knew of John's marriage, for he came to tell me when he had already been wed a twelvemonth. It would have been twenty-six, twenty-seven years ago, for John has been dead these four and twenty years past. Anyway, I was not well pleased, for the Kentons have never been rich and I had hoped he would make an advantageous match.'

'Did you meet John's bride, Sir Thomas?' Frances asked eagerly. She seemed to have recovered her spirits and had picked up her bowl of strawberries again.

Sir Thomas smiled at her. 'No, my dear, I did not. I did not even know her name! I quarrelled with John when he told me of the marriage. To my shame, I admit I threatened to cut him off without a penny! Mere bravado on my part, for I would never have borne such a grudge. Yet I was well served for my anger and pride, for John stormed out of the house and I never saw him again! I later heard that he had gone abroad and died in the Americas, and I wondered what had happened to his bride. I had Knottingley, my man of business, institute a search in Oxford, where John had lodgings, and they said that a lady had left there some months before, but no one knew her direction. She appeared to have no relatives or friends to support her, and the landlady had worried that she was sickly—' He broke off, shaking his head. 'At any rate, we could find no trace of her. I wondered if she would come to us here at Kenton, but she never did so. Often I wondered what had become of her, alone in the world and with John dead. I hoped that she had had family to go to.'

There was a silence.

'I do not understand,' Frances said plaintively. 'If Eliza Hammond had been married for a twelvemonth, why did she not tell her family?'

There was another silence.

'I think perhaps I understand,' Lavender said hesitantly. 'Mr Kenton had married beneath him in choosing a bride who was a maid in your house, Lord Frederick. Neither he nor his wife told their family. I believe they married secretly in Northampton, then moved to Mr Kenton's lodgings in Oxford. It was only when Mrs Kenton discovered that she was expecting a child that her husband decided to approach his family, knowing full well that he had been intended to make an advantageous match.'

Sir Thomas nodded. 'I doubt John could have supported two on his allowance, certainly.' His face fell. 'I fear his worst fears were realised—he came to Kenton and was repudiated. After which he must have hatched a plan to travel abroad and make his fortune.'

'I suppose that Eliza would not have been able to travel with him since she was *enceinte*,' Caroline said thoughtfully, 'but when she was near her time and sickly to boot, she decided to go home to the only place she could, which was Abbot Quincey. I dare say she would not have had the courage to come here—forgive me, Sir Thomas—but she had grown up a mere seven miles away, and so...' Caroline shrugged.

'Then Mr Hammond is your grandson, Sir Thomas,' Frances said after a moment. 'How delightful! He is the most charming young man, and so like your portrait there—' She nodded to Sir Barnabas beside the fireplace.

'Well,' Lewis said, after a pause, 'I suppose that someone should acquaint Mr Hammond of his situation, for surely he is in ignorance of all this—'

'Not precisely...' Lavender shifted uncomfortably in her chair. 'I tried to broach the matter with Mr

Hammond yesterday, but he… I am not sure that he…' She looked around at all the puzzled faces. 'Oh dear. In short, I am not at all sure that he will be pleased by our interference—'

The door opened to admit the same po-faced butler as before. He cleared his throat. 'Sir Thomas, you have two further visitors. Mr James Oliver and Mr Barnabas Hammond.'

'Oh dear,' Lavender said.

It was later, and the Brabants' carriage was rolling homeward in the dusk, carrying Caroline, Lewis and Lavender. The Covinghams' travelling coach was behind and Lavender could well imagine the scenes inside as Lady Anne and Lord Freddie ticked off their recalcitrant daughter. Lewis and Caroline's reproofs had been more measured, but then they probably thought that Lavender had suffered enough. She thought so too.

The look on Barney Hammond's face when he had found them all sitting there in Sir Thomas's library would stay with Lavender for a long time. He had looked directly at her only once, when he had first come in, and there had been such a flash of fury deep in his eyes that Lavender had looked away. Of course she had known that he did not want her to pry any further into his history, but she had thought…hoped…that once he had discovered that his parents had been married and he had a grandfather still living, he would come to her in gratitude. It had not happened and now Lavender was feeling slightly indignant, for surely Barney must see that he would still be just the adopted son of the draper if it were not for her.

Barney had clearly been ill at ease at Kenton and had explained to Sir Thomas that he had only called because he had gone to Hewly and had been told that the whole family and visitors were at Kenton on some urgent errand. Knowing that Miss Brabant had mentioned something of Kenton in connection with his ancestry—here his gaze had touched Lavender's face again, very briefly—he had come there himself to try to resolve the mystery.

At that point, Lavender had been sure that the whole matter was about to be resolved and Barney's love and gratitude pour down on her head. Unfortunately, the Brabants, Covinghams and James Oliver had collectively remembered their manners and decided to withdraw and leave Barney and his grandfather to discuss matters in private. It was all highly unsatisfactory.

Lavender sighed as she watched the darkening country flow past. It seemed she could not do right for doing wrong. She was in trouble with Lewis and Caroline for disappearing without a word and embarrassing them by involving Frances Covingham, and she was in trouble with Barney for delving into his past and digging up a secret for which he did not

seem particularly grateful. As far as she was concerned she would devote herself to her botany in future and leave everyone else to their own devices.

'At the least you could have taken me with you!'
Julia's voice was a petulant wail. 'The whole county
is talking of Sir Thomas Kenton's long-lost grandson, and I could have been there when it happened!
Of all the shabby tricks—to leave me behind!'

Lavender stoically ignored her cousin. She was sitting by the window in the library, trying to catch the
last of the daylight. Unusually, she was sewing an
embroidered shirt for Caroline's baby—a sort of
peace-offering for causing her brother and sister-in-
law so many problems recently. Lavender looked at
the shirt and sighed—she knew she had no talent for
needlework and the collar was distinctly lopsided.

'To think that Mr Hammond is Sir Thomas's heir,'
Julia was saying now, utterly unstoppable once she
had started. 'Heir to Kenton Hall—'

'And to the baronetcy!' Caroline put in slyly.

Julia's face worked like a pan of boiling milk.
'Well, upon my word, fate can be so very unfair! An
estate and a title for the adopted son of a draper!'
She turned on Lavender. 'I'll wager you will be re-
considering your refusal of his suit now, cousin! Lud,
to be Lady Kenton and mistress of the Hall!'

Lavender folded the tiny shirt neatly away. She did

not wish to stay and be the butt of Julia's bad temper, for she knew she would snap at her.

'He still has no money,' she said sharply. 'I thought that that was one of your prerequisites, Julia?'

Julia shrugged. 'Well, he may not be Hammond's heir since he is his nephew rather than his son, but the man is as rich as a nabob and might well do the pretty by him. Besides, with your fortune, Lavender, and Mr Hammond's prospects—'

'It would suddenly become a good bargain?' Lavender snapped. 'I thank you, cousin, but some of us look for more in a match than that! I am scarce likely to forget that a week ago everyone was telling me that it would be the most unequal marriage imaginable!'

Caroline sighed and Julia opened her big blue eyes very wide. 'Well, a week ago that would have been true! Lud, cousin, I do not see your point!'

Lavender slammed out of the library. She could not believe that she was the only one to see the hypocrisy of the situation. Suddenly all those who had put the match down as beneath her were praising it to the skies. It made her furious. Worse was the fact that Barney had not called at Hewly, either to thank her for her help or to repeat those offers he had made to her so recently. So the matter of a wedding was an academic one now anyway, since he had not proposed.

Lavender was in such a thoroughly bad mood by the time that she went out for a walk, that not even the beautiful evening could soothe her. The moon was rising above the forest and a breeze was rustling the autumn leaves. There was the scent of grass and smoke and the river rippled in the moonlight, secret and silver. Lavender paused to watch it eddy and flow and tried to find some peace in her heart.

She sat for a long time on a large flat stone on the bank, listening to the rustle of mice in the grass and the plop of fish in the river, and when she heard a step on the path behind her she did not need to turn her head to know who was there.

'Mr Hammond! How is it that you are forever skulking in the woods, sir!'

'I am sorry,' Barney's voice came out of the semi-darkness, not sounding particularly apologetic. 'In point of fact, I was not skulking but coming to Hewly to see you, Miss Brabant!'

'At this time of night?' Lavender knew she sounded sulky but she could not help herself. She had waited for days for him to call and now that he was finally there she had a perverse desire to be horrid to him.

'May I sit down?' Barney did not wait for her permission but settled himself on the rock beside her. 'I wanted to speak to you—'

'Did you?' Lavender snapped. 'I have grown tired of the waiting, sir!'

'Perhaps you thought I should come to thank you ere now?' Barney asked. He sounded amused. His arm brushed hers and Lavender moved pointedly away. She could feel his warmth, feel herself relaxing and leaning towards him. His presence undermined her defences.

'A show of gratitude would have been appreciated—'

'Ah, but you see I was very angry with you!' Barney still sounded amused. 'I had asked you most particularly not to interfere in my case and then I find that not only have you discussed me with your family and friends, but you have also taken it upon yourself to go to Kenton and to see Sir Thomas! First you ignore my express wishes and then I find I am beholden to you yet again—'

Lavender felt the indignant colour rush into her face then rush away again. This was not at all what she had expected. To be reprimanded when surely he owed her the biggest debt of gratitude imaginable! 'Well, upon my word! And I was expecting your thanks rather than your reproaches! You and your foolish pride! Are you not pleased to have found your grandfather and an estate and title into the bargain?'

It was not at all what was important to her, but she was so cross with him that she wanted to hit back. And having seen some evidence of his temper before, she knew that it was possible to provoke him.

It did not seem to work this time, however, for
Barney laughed.

'Oh, I am most happy to meet my grandfather, for
I like him prodigiously and I think—hope—that he
likes me too! As for the rest, well, I have had plenty
of people tell me over the past week that I should be
grateful for my prospects, but I did not expect you
to be one of them, Miss Brabant! I seem to recall
that you swore you loved me even when I had nothing to offer you! It is strange to see you value
worldly possessions so highly now!'

Lavender jumped up, stung. She did not want to
be reminded of declarations of love when she felt so
out of charity with him. 'Oh, I do not care two pins
for your fortune, but I think you should acknowledge
that it is as a result of my persistence that you are in
this situation! If I had heeded your strictures and left
well alone you would never have known of your parentage or your inheritance! And under the circumstances it seems to me ungrateful that you cannot
give me that credit!'

Barney had also stood up now and was moving
towards her with a deliberation that made Lavender
suddenly nervous. She took a hasty step back, stumbled and would have fallen in the river had Barney
not caught her arm.

'Careful, Miss Brabant! You will tumble into the
water in a minute and then I shall be put to the trouble of fishing you out!'

'Oh!' Lavender stamped her foot. 'Let go, you odious man! I do not want you, nor your estate, nor your title, and I am sorry I ever interfered to find your family for you! I wish I had left you to struggle in the shop!'

Barney pulled her into his arms and before she could protest her lips were crushed beneath his in a kiss that drove all the remaining breath from her body. If her comment had been outrageous then she considered his behaviour to be no less so. When he let her go she wanted to berate him, but found that instead she needed to hold on to him to steady herself whilst the ground settled beneath her feet again and the stars stopped swinging in their courses. Barney did not seem to mind. He held her close and pressed his lips to her hair.

'Come, Lavender, let us put this foolish quarrelling behind us! Say that you will marry me, now that I do at least have something to offer you…'

Lavender could hear the smile in his voice. The press of his body against hers was infinitely distracting. She tried to clear her mind.

'You may remember, sir, that when you asked me to marry you before, I was willing—happy—to do so, and no consideration of rank or station entered into the matter. So I would not wish to be influenced by them, now that your circumstances have changed. No, I am sorry, I will not marry you.'

She felt Barney go still, then his arms loosened

and he stepped back from her. The chill evening air wrapped round her, filling the space where his warmth had been.

'Lavender, you know that my reluctance had nothing to do with my feelings and stemmed only from an awareness of the inequality of our situation—'

Lavender backed away. 'I know it. Yet I did not share your reluctance. I would have been happy to marry you and live on nothing in a cottage! I loved you enough to do so!'

Barney grimaced. 'Lavender, that is not fair! I was thinking only of you—the wretchedness of asking you to give everything up to marry me! Now I have so much more to offer—'

'And I do not want it!' Lavender said. 'All I wanted was you, but that was not good enough for you! So now that you have so much more the answer is still no!'

The tears came into her eyes and she dashed them away. 'I understand your pride and your reluctance. You did not want to offer for me before, when you felt you had nothing. I even understand that you might feel angry to be indebted to me for finding your link to the Kentons, although truly I consider that the greatest thanklessness!' Her voice was husky and she cleared her throat. 'What you forget, sir, is that I too have my pride! All that I have ever done has been to help you, and I do not see why I should fall in with your plans now, just because it suits your purpose! So—no—I shall not marry you!'

And once again she ran from him and did not look back.

Chapter Eleven

'This is most unfortunate!' Caroline sighed. It was the following morning and Lavender had just confessed to Caroline and Lewis that Barney had proposed again and she had still refused him.

'You are an unconscionably stubborn girl, Lavender!' Lewis said irritably. 'I cannot think where you get it from! Surely you must see that Mr Hammond is trying to do what is right and has been doing so since the very beginning!'

'I don't care!' Lavender knew she sounded petulant. 'I wanted to marry Barney when he had nothing to his name, but he did not wish it then! Just because he will one day be Sir Barnabas—well, a fine fortune-hunter I shall appear if I suddenly turn around and say that I will take him after all!'

'Well, that may be what people will say,' Caroline said fairly, 'but what does that matter? Surely the point is that you are in love with him, and that he loves you, and as such you would be foolish not to make a match of it!'

Lavender turned her face away. 'I do not wish to talk of it! I shall take my paints out and do some sketches for my book! I have no wish to stay here for your chiding, or to hear Julia going on about how the carriages are lined up outside Kenton Hall with all the eligible girls in the neighbourhood angling to be the next Lady Kenton!'

Lewis laughed and Lavender thought him quite heartless. 'I hear that Julia is to leave us soon, at any rate!' he said cheerfully. 'Poor Lady Leverstoke has passed away and I'll wager Julia is coming out of her seclusion to snap up Charles Leverstoke before anyone else gets there first!'

Caroline laughed. She put down the letter she was reading. 'And Anne Covingham writes that she and Sir Freddie have relented of their opposition to Frances's attachment to James Oliver, so matters there seem set fair! Now Lavender, if only you could settle your differences with Mr Hammond we may all be comfortable!'

'I think you are both disgusting!' Lavender snapped. 'I am shocked that you seek to encourage me to marry just for material gain! I am going out!'

And she stormed out of the room, leaving Lewis and Caroline looking at each other in amused resignation.

* * *

Lavender did not feel much better when she returned to Hewly for luncheon to find that the house was empty and Lewis and Caroline were away visiting. The morning had not been at all as she had planned: She had been stung by nettles and had dropped her sketching book in a stream so that her carefully illustrated pictures of Herb Robert had run all over the page. Feeling cross-grained and irritable, she took luncheon alone and was just silently chewing a cold collation when there was a knock at the door and Rosie came in. She bobbed a curtsey.

'Begging your pardon, Miss Lavender, but the carriage is here from Kenton Hall. There is a man with a message from Sir Thomas. He asks that you join him there immediately. It is a matter of extreme urgency, he says.'

Lavender put down her fork. 'A matter of urgency?'

'So Sir Thomas's servant says, ma'am. And he has sent the carriage especially—'

Lavender frowned. After her last escapade she had no inclination to go travelling on a whim and letting herself open to Lewis and Caroline's condemnation as a result. On the other hand, Sir Thomas was asking for her and the matter was evidently important enough that he had sent his carriage specially. She went over to the window and pulled back the drapes. Sure enough, a coach with the Kenton arms was standing beside the door and an ostler was holding the horses' heads and talking to one of the Hewly grooms. Lavender let the curtain fall back into place.

'Oh, very well. Tell the man I shall be ready in ten minutes.'

She scribbled a quick note for Caroline and Lewis, making it crystal clear that the invitation had come from Sir Thomas and was no mad start of her own, then ran upstairs to wash her hands and fetch a fresh bonnet. Her lavender blue dress had a stain on it where she had knelt down to rescue her sketchbook from the stream, but she did not feel she had the time to change. As it was, the horses were scraping the gravel when she went outside, and they set off without further ado.

It was only as they neared Kenton that Lavender was suddenly struck by the impropriety of her own actions. Last time she had been accompanied by Frances, which had been bad enough in its own way, but this time she had not even brought a maid with her. She was so accustomed to wandering about Hewly and Steep Wood at will that she seldom gave any thought to the danger she might be in, but now she wondered with a little stab of despair whether she would ever learn to go on as she ought. Her overwrought nerves prompted her to believe that the invitation might have been part of a kidnap plot, and she was just imagining all kinds of Gothic horrors when the carriage turned in at the gates of Kenton Hall and started up the drive.

It was immediately clear that some kind of transformation had already begun to take place. Men had been working in the deer park, cutting the grass beneath the trees and weeding the drive, but on this drowsy afternoon the gardens were as silent as they had been the previous week. The carriage pulled up outside the main entrance and the groom respectfully held the door for Lavender to dismount. She looked around for Sir Thomas, but it was his grandson whom she saw coming forward from the stables, the sleeves of his shirt rolled up to show that he had been working when she arrived. Lavender stared.

'You! But I thought—'

The coach rolled off into the yard and Barney came forward to take Lavender's hand.

'Thank you for responding to my invitation so promptly, Miss Brabant!'

Lavender blinked. 'I beg your pardon, sir. I thought it was Sir Thomas who had sent the message—'

Barney shrugged gracefully. 'I fear my grandfather is from home at present and it was I who sent the summons in his name! An unchivalrous deception, but I feared you might refuse if you knew the invitation was from me!'

He held the door for her and after a moment, Lavender followed him into the hall. Here, as outside, there were remarkable changes. The windows were open, letting in the cool autumn air, the furniture had been polished to a high gloss and all the curtains and carpets cleaned.

'My grandfather felt it appropriate to have the house spring-cleaned, for all that it is autumn!' Barney said, a little awkwardly.

Lavender smiled. 'Perhaps he felt that, despite the turning of the year, it was time for a fresh start?'

'Yes, perhaps.' Barney smiled back. 'Would you like to see more?'

Lavender agreed, a little hesitantly. She was curious as to why Barney had lured her to Kenton, but she found to her surprise that she did not resent it. Rather, a strange feeling of warmth had stolen over her when she had seen him coming forward to greet her. She was pleased to see him and she could not deny it. Everything had seemed wrong after their last quarrel, the balance of things quite upset, and she had had no idea how it could ever be put right again. She had been cross and bad-tempered without him but she did not want him to know that—at least, not quite yet.

They admired the library, where the portraits were in the process of being cleaned, then strolled out through the terrace doors into the gardens. It was even quieter than before.

'So your grandfather is away—but where are all the servants?' Lavender asked, looking round. 'There has been so much activity here that I quite expected to see them hard at their tasks!'

Barney laughed. 'I have given everyone the afternoon off! As you say, they have been working so hard that they deserve it!'

'And you have been working hard too, by the looks of things!' Lavender smiled. 'Have you been staying here at Kenton?'

'Yes, I have been staying with my grandfather—' Barney still brought the phrase out hesitantly '—these three days past, and he has suggested that I move to Kenton Hall as soon as may be convenient. There is much for me to learn of the estate and the farms and—' Barney broke off, shaking his head. 'It still seems quite extraordinary!'

'Do you like Sir Thomas?' Lavender asked hesitantly. 'When we met before you said that you did!'

Barney gave her his sudden smile. 'Oh, prodigiously! To tell the truth, I was not entirely happy about the discovery of my new situation—' he slanted a look down at her '—which was one of the reasons why I was so ungrateful when you sprang the surprise of my inheritance on me! I had so many plans relating to my study of pharmacology and no wish to give them up... Anyway, Sir Thomas feels that need not signify and that I may continue my work at Kenton, so perhaps I shall achieve my ambition eventually and join the Royal Pharmaceutical Society! I confess it is a relief to think that it will not all be gentlemanly pursuits and that my work may feature somewhere!'

Lavender laughed. 'To think that so many people might envy you, sir, and that you secretly hanker for your experiments and your studies!'

Barney pulled a face. 'Disgraceful ingratitude, I know! But I had worked so hard and always wished to achieve success through my own merit!'

'Which is admirable,' Lavender conceded, 'but it will not make you turn your back on your inheritance, I hope?'

'No,' Barney was smiling. 'I would be foolish indeed not to see the benefits that that entails, and there is no point in struggling unnecessarily! Besides, Sir Thomas deserves better than that—having found a grandson so late in life he does not deserve to lose him twice!'

Lavender blinked a little, ashamed of the tears that prickled her eyes. 'I am so glad, for he is such a nice man!' She smiled. 'How has your uncle taken your good fortune?'

Barney grinned. 'Oh, he is well pleased! In fact I do believe he wishes it had all occurred sooner, and then he would have been on calling terms with Kenton Hall these five and twenty years past!'

Lavender smiled to think how happy the social climbing Arthur Hammond would be now. To have a nephew connected with the landed gentry was more than he could ever have imagined.

Barney took her hand. 'Lavender, forgive me for bringing you here under false pretences, but I needed

to speak to you in private. I have proposed to you
on two occasions and have no intention of making a
third declaration! I should tell you that I rode over
to Hewly this morning and obtained your brother's
permission—a second time—to marry you, and that
he and Mrs Brabant wished me the best of good luck
against your stubborn nature! So I do not intend to
beat about the bush! You are to marry me three
weeks hence. Sir Thomas has arranged for the banns
to be read here at Kenton and is delighted that there
is to be a family wedding after so long a time. All it
requires is your consent!'

Lavender stared at him, affronted. She was not
sure what rankled more, Lewis and Caroline's per-
fidious betrayal or Barney's high-handedness when
she had expected a pretty proposal. She freed her
hand from his and stepped back.

'You presume a great deal, sir! How if I do not
wish to be married?'

'It makes no odds,' Barney said implacably. 'In
the first place, you told me several weeks ago that
you were in love with me, so I am no coxcomb to
remind you of it! Secondly I do not believe that you
wish to remain a spinster! That may well suit others,
but it will not do for you! Come, Lavender, why do
you not consent? You could live here at Kenton and
still study your botany… You know you would like
it…'

Lavender did like the idea of it and it rankled with

her to have to admit it. She turned her back on him and started to walk down the path towards the courtyard. She had no clear idea of where she was going but she hoped that Barney might come after her and follow his proposal up with a sweeter persuasion. She knew she was being stubborn and she was even more annoyed when Barney did not follow her to press ardent words of love on her, but sauntered along at some distance behind, whistling.

Lavender began to feel a little foolish. She reached the stableyard, hoping that the carriage might be waiting and she could prevail upon one of the grooms to take her back to Hewly. However, there was no one about. She peered into a barn stacked high with hay, and turned to see Barney standing in the doorway and laughing at her.

'Lavender, when will you stop running away? I told you that you are here at Kenton alone with me!'

Lavender raised her eyebrows. 'Oh surely, sir, you cannot mean to suggest that my reputation is in danger! It is lost already, if you recall—'

'Ah yes…' Barney smiled, moving closer. 'So you are implying that you are already irreparably compromised by me and cannot fall any further! I think that a mistake—'

Before Lavender could read his intention, he had taken hold of her wrist and pulled her down into the hay.

'You suggested before that I had spent my time

tumbling village girls in haystacks,' Barney said. 'Well, it was not true, but I am happy to remedy the situation now!' He rolled Lavender over on to her back and pinned her down in the hay.

'Let me up!' Lavender cried, sneezing as the hay tickled her nose. 'This is absurd, sir—'

'Then agree to marry me!'

Lavender struggled, threshing around in the straw and succeeding in doing nothing other than lose her bonnet. 'There must be any number of women who would wish to be Lady Kenton of Kenton Hall!'

'I daresay, but I want this one! Lavender, I love you! Must you be so difficult?'

Lavender lay still and looked up into the dark eyes so very close to her own. She put out a hand to touch his cheek. 'I am not sure…' she murmured.

Barney took her hand in his, turned it over and kissed the palm. 'Then I must make you sure,' he said huskily. 'Where had we got to, that day at Steepwood Pool? Ah, I remember… Your hair was tumbled all about you…' He paused to look at her, 'just as it is now. And your dress…' His fingers moved to the buttons at her neck.

Lavender slapped his hand aside. 'Barney! What are you doing—'

Barney looked at her expressively. He was shrugging off his jacket and untying his stock. 'I would have thought that that is obvious! I am seducing you in order to force you to marry me!' He pulled his shirt over his head with an impatient gesture. 'Oh, and also because I wish to do so!'

Lavender sat up abruptly, just as he leant over her again. The movement brought her palms up against the smooth brown skin of his chest and she lay back with a little gasp.

'Oh! Surely you cannot be serious! There is no need to seduce me!'

'You disappoint me.' Barney's breath stirred a tendril of hair as his lips drifted across the soft skin below her ear. They moved on to brush her mouth, lightly, teasingly, before withdrawing. 'So you will marry me?'

'Yes,' Lavender whispered, pinned to the spot by the heat in his eyes. 'Oh yes, I will…'

'Good,' Barney sounded brisk, but he lowered his mouth to hers again with lazy sensuality. 'We shall seal our bargain,' he said, against her mouth.

His lips teased hers apart, deepening the kiss until Lavender's head spun and the blood burned hot in her veins. When Barney's fingers returned to the neck of her gown and started to undo the row of buttons at her throat, she did not resist but tried to help, clumsy in her eagerness. The material parted, and as Barney bent to kiss the hollow of her throat, Lavender ran her hands over his shoulders, pulling him closer, revelling in the velvet hardness of the muscles beneath his skin.

It was not long before they were exactly as they

had been beside Steepwood Pool, Lavender in her shift, speechless with desire as Barney unlaced the bodice to slip his hands inside and cup her breasts. The yielding hay surrounded her, filling her senses with the hazy, fruitful smell of summer, a scent that mingled with her desire and made her light-headed with need. She wriggled the shift down to her waist, arching against Barney so that her breasts were pressed against his chest as she raised her mouth for his kiss again. He drank deep of her and she could sense his need, barely held in check. Her questing fingers stole down to his waist and tugged at his breeches, seeking the fastening.

'A moment—' His impatience matched hers. She could hear it in his voice, feel it in the tension of his body. Lavender closed her eyes as he moved to pull the trousers off, then opened them wide again as he followed his own divesting with hers. A belated modesty made her clutch the shift and drawers to her nakedness, but Barney prised them from her fingers, covering the coolness of her bare skin with the warmth of his own at the same time as his mouth covered hers. She felt his hand on her thigh, and shifted to accommodate his body with her own. There was the most intolerable ache within her and she longed for him to appease it with his body on hers, and even as she thought it, he was inside her and the pleasure filled her and she cried aloud.

They lay still for a long time afterwards, clasped

in each other's arms, half-hidden in the hay. Eventually Barney stirred, pushed the tumbled hair back from Lavender's face and kissed her slowly, drawing out the pleasure. He allowed his hands to travel over her in triumphant possession, sliding over her hips, tracing the curve of her breasts. Lavender made a little noise of contentment, pulling him back into her arms.

'Who would have thought it would be so pleasurable,' she murmured.

'Not I, certainly.' Barney's face was pressed against her neck and she could feel him smiling against her skin. 'Is it better than painting?'

'Oh, far better!'

'Or botany?'

Lavender stretched, raising her arms above her head. Barney let go of her a little, but only so that he could bend over her and kiss her again. Lavender squirmed.

'Barney—'

'You were flaunting your exquisite body and how could I resist?'

'Exquisite…' Lavender thought, warmed suddenly by pride and something else. Suddenly Barney's hands were on her waist again, pulling her close to him again. The tide of passion swept over them.

'Barney—' Lavender gasped, spun up in the sensations of the moment.

'I said that you would prefer to be married,'

Barney said later, lazily. They were lying entwined in the hay again, unable to move far away from each other. 'Unless, of course—' his mouth brushed hers '—you do not wish to marry me now?'

In response, Lavender snuggled closer and they lay quiet again until the clock on the stables chimed the hour. Barney stirred and said:

'I imagine my grandfather may be back soon, and the servants are returning this evening so perhaps we should get up—'

Lavender let out a little shriek and sat bolt upright, casting around desperately for her clothes. 'Oh no! If Sir Thomas finds me here, he will scarce consider me a suitable bride for his grandson!'

Barney pulled her back down into his arms. 'I think you suitable, and that is what matters. So, are we to make our unequal match?'

Lavender smiled into his eyes. 'With all my heart,' she said.

*   *   *   *   *

Modern Romance™
...seduction and
passion guaranteed

Tender Romance™
...love affairs that
last a lifetime

Sensual Romance™
...sassy, sexy and
seductive

Blaze
...sultry days and
steamy nights

Medical Romance™
...medical drama on
the pulse

Historical Romance™
...rich, vivid and
passionate

29 new titles every month.

*With all kinds of Romance for
every kind of mood...*

MILLS & BOON®

Makes any time special™

MAT4

READER SERVICE™

The best romantic fiction direct to your door

Our guarantee to you...

The Reader Service involves you in no obligation to purchase, and is truly a service to you!

There are many extra benefits including a free monthly Newsletter with author interviews, book previews and much more.

Your books are sent direct to your door on 14 days no obligation home approval.

We offer huge discounts on selected books exclusively for subscribers.

Plus, we have a dedicated Customer Care team on hand to answer all your queries on
(UK) 020 8288 2888
(Ireland) 01 278 2062.

Tender Romance™
6 brand new titles each month
...love affairs
that last a lifetime
Available on subscription every month
from the Reader Service™
GEN/02/RS2

Sensual Romance™
4 brand new titles each month
...sassy, sexy and seductive.
Available on subscription every month from the Reader Service™
GEN/21/RS2